CHARLOTTE

Brides of the Oregon Trail, Book 6

CYNTHIA WOOLF

CHAPTER ONE

Outside Oregon City, December 2, 1854

Charlotte Taylor, sat atop her horse, Gulliver, her latest kill, a small doe, tied to the saddle behind her. Her rifle was in its scabbard, her knife was in her boot as always and her gun belt held two pistols. A cold December breeze made her glad for her heavy sheepskin coat and the lined leather riding gloves. Sitting at the top of the hill watching over the wooden and brick buildings that made up her town, her home, her chest filled with pride.

She loved Oregon City. Sure she wouldn't when they arrived with the wagon train a year ago, she was wrong. There were things she'd change like their acceptance of her wearing pants, but even that wasn't from everyone, mostly just a couple of old biddies who liked to have bad things to say about everyone and gossip about anyone.

Now, she turned Gulliver, her big Appaloosa stallion, to face downhill so she could watch the city fellow on the bay mare, whose coat was barely enough to keep the wind from whipping through. He was riding back and forth through the trees and she figured he must be lost. She looked him over and sized him up. *Probably about six feet, maybe an inch or two taller, lean, muscular if the pulling of the shoulders of his jacket are any indication. Dark hair. Moustache. Handsome in a citified sort of way.*

He must be looking for the road. He'll never find it like that. I suppose I should go help him.

She rode down the hill and stopped about twenty feet from him. "Lost?"

He looked up as she approached. "Yes, it would appear so. I pulled off the road for a moment to...well suffice it to say, I needed to pull off the road. But I seem to have gotten myself turned around. Can you point me in the direction of the road to Oregon City?"

"I will." She leaned forward resting her arms on the saddle horn. "For a dollar."

His eyes widened, then narrowed and he smiled. "Well played. You have me over a barrel, Miss..."

"Charlie. Charlie Taylor."

"Charlie Taylor. That's a rather unusual name for a woman as is the way you are dressed. I've never seen a woman wearing pants and pistols before. But, unusual or not, you do have me somewhat at your mercy, so you have a deal. You show me the way to Oregon City and I'll give you a dollar."

Charlie nodded. "Follow me." She turned and walked Gulliver back up the hill. At the top she stopped and waited for him.

When he reined his mount in next to her, his mouth fell open and he turned to her, eyebrow cocked.

"You couldn't tell me to go to the top of the hill?"

She shrugged. "I could have but what fun would that be? Who are you, by the way?"

"Travis MacGregor, Esquire at your service." He dipped his head and leaned forward resting his arms on the saddle horn. "I'm here to visit a friend of mine. Maybe you know him? Ian Stanton is his name. Got married last year."

Charlie thought of her new brother-in-law, Ian, who married her sister Rebecca last year and laughed. "Esquire, huh? And just what does that mean?" *I know you Mr. Travis MacGregor, Esquire. Our paper ran a big story about how you go into companies, tear them apart and sell them, without a care about what happens to the employees of the company. I want you to see who you're hurting. You're about to meet all my kids. Oh, yes, come with me said the spider to the bee.*

"Only that I'm a lawyer."

"All right. And where are you from, Travis MacGregor, Esquire?"

"Philadelphia. I'm here—"

She stopped him not wanting to hear the reason he

was here. Not wanting to hear the name of the business he came to destroy. "I know. You're here to see Ian. I'll take you to him after we make a stop."

"Thank you."

She leaned over and put out her hand. "You owe me a dollar."

He shook his head and laughed, but he reached into his pocket and pulled out a silver coin. "Here you go."

Charlie put the money in her vest then patted the pocket. "Come see my town."

They rode down the hill into town and she led him to the Oregon City Mercantile. They dismounted and went inside.

Charlie walked up to the counter where Ernest Duncanson was behind the counter. The man, with brown hair that was thinning on the top and wearing a white apron, greeted her as she approached.

"Well, hi there, Charlie. I wondered when I'd be seeing you this week."

"Hi, Ernest, this here is Travis MacGregor. He's new here. I'm taking him to see Ian, but I need my regular order first."

"I got it packed up right here."

He handed her a small paper sack from under the counter.

"Thanks. Here you go." She placed the dollar Travis had given her on the counter. "See you later." She turned to Travis. "Let's go. I got things to do at home."

Outside on the boardwalk, she stopped, put her

thumb and forefinger in her mouth and blew out a shrill, loud whistle.

Travis started at the unexpected sound. "What the heck?"

She ignored him and watched with a smile as suddenly, from all over the town, kids came running, thirty or forty of them, depending on the day of the week.

"Charlie." Some of the kids shouted as they came forward.

Several others hugged her and one even carried a baby.

"Edgar, you know Janie can't have candy yet and you don't get extra for bringing her, even as cute as she is." She reached down, tickled the baby under the chin and got a wide, toothless smile for her efforts.

"Hi, Janie baby. How are you today?" She kissed the top of the baby's head.

The little boy looked crestfallen and then he grinned. "Can't blame a kid for tryin'."

She turned to Travis. "These kids' daddies work as lumberjacks for the various owners of the tree lands or at the sawmill."

She handed a little boy a stick of candy. "This is Johnny, his daddy works at the saw mill."

A little girl with blonde braids and freckles across her nose and cheeks walked up. "Can I have one for my daddy?"

Charlie reached into the bag. "You sure can, sugarplum. You tell him I said hi, okay?"

The girl nodded and, after she got the candy, trotted away.

"That was Sarah. Her daddy was a lumberjack. He fell last year and broke both his legs. He's just now getting back to walking, but he'll never climb trees again. He's been training with Mr. Caldwell to work in the bank. We try to take care of our own."

"Why are you showing me these children and telling me about their fathers?"

"Because there was a story about you in the newspaper, all the way here from New York. I wanted you to see the face of the people before you started your job."

Each child got a stick of candy until only a few remained to take home to her little brothers and sister. Ian's twin boys became her little brothers when he'd married her sister, Rebecca, a year ago. But she wasn't telling Travis that. She wanted to see his reaction when she took him to Ian.

She waited until the last child ran away. "All right, we can go now."

He waved his hand after the last child. "That's what you wanted my dollar for? Candy for the kids?"

She nodded and started walking toward the hitching rail where the horses were tied. "Yup. I try to do it once a week. A lot of these kids don't get sweets very often and nothing like a candy stick except maybe at Christmas. It's something I can do to make their lives a little better."

He looked down and then back at her. "That's a very nice thing you do."

Smiling, the praise feeling good, she jutted her chin toward the horses. "Thanks. Shall we go? I'll take you to Ian."

He nodded. "Let's go. I haven't seen him for more than seven years now. He hadn't married Molly yet when I saw him last and now he's married to Rebecca. I can't wait to meet the woman who won his heart."

Charlie smiled. Ian had mentioned Travis when that story came out about him and his firm's practice of going in, gutting a business and selling off the assets, while leaving the employees decimated and unemployed. Travis would be even more irritated with her when he found out Ian was her brother-in-law, which made it even more delicious and her smile wider. The man deserved to be irritated and more.

They pulled up to the hitching rail in front of the big three story house. The house had just gotten the last coat of pretty blue paint which was a great improvement over the weathered gray it was before.

"Come on in." She headed up the porch to the front door, smacking her riding gloves on her pants.

He followed her and then came abreast of her at the door. He put his hand on her arm. "Come in? Do you live here? I thought you were taking me to Ian."

She looked down at his hand on her arm.

He removed it.

"I am. Come in."

Travis followed her into the house.

Charlie shouted when she entered. "Ian, you have company." She turned to Travis. "Sorry, he could be anywhere in the house working on something and I don't want to go from room to room." The unmistakable scent of lacquer or wood stain permeated the air.

"Oh, Ian works here. Well that explains things."

She had to bite her lip to keep from laughing. Then she heard footsteps on the stairs.

"What did you say, Charlie? Who's here?"

Travis looked up and faced Ian.

Ian got the biggest smile on his face and ran down the stairs to his friend. "Travis! How are you? What are you doing here? Based on your last letter, I didn't think you'd be able to come." He wrapped the man in a bear hug that was returned.

Charlie had been wrong in her assessment of the man's height. He was about two inches taller than Ian, which would put him at about six four. Interesting. If she'd been interested in men at all, he would probably be her type. If she had a type.

Her interest in men, in getting married was killed the first time she saw her father beat her mother and her mother unable to do anything about it. Charlie made sure that would never happen to her. She bought her guns with her first two paychecks and then she learned how to use them...well, very well.

Ian turned his gaze on her. "Thanks for bringing him home. He was probably lost. The man has no sense of direction. Never has."

Travis reddened.

Charlie burst out laughing. She just couldn't hold it in anymore.

"What?" asked Ian as he raised one brow in question?

"I have to admit I played a joke on your friend. I didn't tell him you're my brother-in-law and that this is our house. I let him think you just worked here." She chuckled some more.

Travis took off his hat and ran a hand through his hair. "Do you have to be right all the time?" he asked Ian.

"What is going on in here?"

Rebecca entered from the kitchen, carrying baby Grace. "Let's move to the parlor where we can be more comfortable. She led them into the room adjacent to the entry way. Rebecca sat on the blue flowered brocade sofa.

Ian took one of the overstuffed chairs upholstered in a solid blue fabric and facing the sofa.

Travis sat in the chair matching Ian's.

Charlie walked over to Rebecca and smiled down at the four-month-old baby. "Hi, Gracie. Are you being a good baby for Mama? Hmmm? Here, let me have her. You can visit with our company."

"Yes." Ian held his arm out toward Travis. "This is

my friend Travis MacGregor. He and I grew up together and then went to the same college in Philadelphia for a couple of years."

Travis leaned over the coffee table, his right hand extended. "I'm very happy to meet you, Mrs. Stanton."

"Oh, please, I'm Rebecca." She took his hand and then nodded her head toward Charlie. "Have you met my sister Charlotte?"

Charlie frowned at her sister whose brown hair was the total opposite of Charlie's sun-streaked blonde hair and whose deep blue eyes now sparkled with mischief. "Charlie. And yes we've met. He probably wishes we hadn't though. I took him with me to do my weekly candy giveaway and made sure he knew what each child's father did."

Travis smiled. "On the contrary, I never wish I hadn't met a beautiful woman."

"Hmpft." She moved away with the baby toward the stairs, carpeted with the same blue carpet as the entryway and hall to the kitchen. "You probably say that to everyone."

He chuckled. "Only the ornery ones. And I found your introductions of the children very interesting."

Charlie rolled her eyes. "Oh, please, you don't need to flatter me. I brought you home. My good deed for the day is done. I'll take Gracie upstairs." She sniffed the baby. "She needs changing."

"Charlie," said Rebecca. "Before you go why don't you show Travis to the guest room, since you're headed upstairs anyway?" She turned to Travis. "You'll stay with us as long as you're here."

"Thank you, dear lady, but that could be a long time as I am relocating here."

He could be staying here! That will make it very hard to avoid him, but I intend to do my best.

Ian clapped Travis on the back. "That is wonderful news. I'll show you up to the guest room. Charlie can take care of Gracie, who definitely needs changing." He waved his hand in front of him.

Charlie laughed at Ian's antics and took Gracie upstairs.

Ian and Travis followed.

She could feel Travis' gaze on her as she climbed the stairs. She should probably be irritated but she wasn't. What did that mean? She took Gracie to the master bedroom and laid her on top of the short chest of drawers. Ian had fashioned sides on it so she couldn't roll off and added padding so it was comfortable. In the drawers underneath were her diapers and clothes, washcloths and towels. On one side of the dresser was a bucket for the dirty diaper, with a piece of wood to cover the top. On a small table on the other side was a pitcher of water and a basin to wash her from.

"I'm cleaning you up, Gracie. You'll be nice and clean for Mr. MacGregor to hold you. Would you like that?" She tickled Grace's tummy. "Hmm, Gracie. Would you like that?"

Charlie looked at the ceiling. From the room above

she heard the other children playing. They must be playing something with soldiers since it sounded like they were marching.

When Charlie was done with the water in the basin, she poured it in the diaper pail. When the pail was full, it was taken downstairs and the diapers were boiled, rinsed and hung on the outside line to dry. Or if it was rainy, on a line strung on the wall behind the stove.

She heard the footsteps of the men as they headed back downstairs from the guest room which was across the hall.

"There you go Gracie. All clean. Shall we go see your mama and daddy and that handsome friend of your daddy's? Don't tell anyone I think he's handsome. He'll get a big head on his shoulders and I think he already has one."

She took the baby downstairs where she found everyone in the kitchen.

"Travis have you eaten." Rebecca poured him a cup of coffee. "I heard Ian say you were lost so you're probably starving if you were lost for any length of time since leaving Portland. We're about to have lunch. You'll join us or did you have something else you must do?"

"I'll be looking for office space and a place to live but not right now. My assistant Lois Lattimer is coming with the rest of our furnishings."

"Lois?" asked Ian. "Your assistant is a woman?"

"Yes. Her father is a powerful attorney in Philadelphia. I clerked for him while I was in school, then when I started my own practice, Lois began to come and help me." Travis sipped his coffee.

Charlie sat across the table from Travis, Gracie at her shoulder. "I would have thought she would stay in Philadelphia. Wouldn't she have more opportunities there?"

Travis shook his head. "Just the opposite."

"I imagine that's true. No law firm wants to be the first to officially have a female working there as an assistant." said Ian.

"That's right. No one said anything to her father because he was so powerful and they ignored me because I was new at the game."

Rebecca placed sliced roast beef, bread, mayonnaise, and butter on the table, along with plates and eating utensils. "Please make your sandwiches. I also have some potato salad which I'll get as soon as the children are taken care of."

The sound of running children came from the hall. Three little ones burst into the kitchen.

Rebecca shook her finger at them. "Slow down all of you. What have I told you about running in the house?"

The children hung their heads. "No running. Running is for outdoors," they recited together

"That's right. Now, walk quietly to the table and take your seats."

"Yes, ma'am," said Andy, black hair like his father's hung in a single curl over his forehead.

"Okay," said Freddy, was an exact duplicate of Andy

and both of them looked just like Ian. Charlie felt sorry for the girls when those two grew up.

"Yes, Becca," said Carrie Ann, who was the spitting image of Charlie with deep, dark blue eyes and blonde hair. The rest of the siblings, Rebecca, Ben and Peter all had brown hair, but the dark blue eyes was a trait that all of them shared.

Carrie Ann seated herself next to Travis.

"Who are you?" she asked. That was Carrie Ann, friendly to everyone, as long as she was safe. Since her kidnapping last year, she'd been afraid to play in the yard and was shy with strangers outside the house. Charlie thought that maybe Carrie Ann figured someone in the house and sitting at the table to eat with them was safe.

He smiled at her little sister, which added to his attractiveness. She liked people who were kind to children. "I'm Travis. Who are you?"

She put her hands, folded, on the table behind her plate. "I'm Carrie Ann."

"Is Rebecca your mama?"

Carrie Ann shook her head. "Nope. Becca is my sister. She's Gracie's mama."

"I see." He looked up at Ian, eyebrows lifted.

Charlie chuckled. She could imagine just how their family dynamics sounded to someone from the outside.

"Let me see if I can explain," said Rebecca. "Carrie Ann is my baby sister. Our mother died when she was born, so Ben and I raised her. Ben is my twin brother. Here he is now."

"Looks like we have company." Ben extended his right hand. "I'm Ben Taylor. My family and I farm this land."

Travis looked back and forth between Rebecca and Ben.

Ben laughed. "We don't look anything alike."

"Anyway," continued Rebecca. "Carrie Ann is like a daughter to me. We also have a brother, Peter, who is fifteen now and should be here shortly."

"He's taking care of the animals and he'll be in after that." Ben sat at the other end of the table opposite Ian.

Travis looked over at Ben and back to Rebecca across the table from him.

He looked over at Rebecca. "You're correct you two look nothing alike."

"She's very happy she doesn't look like me and so is Ian. We're fraternal twins.," laughed Ben.

Travis chuckled. "I'm sure he is."

Ben and Rebecca always got the same reaction from people who found out they were twins. And usually, they looked a second time at Charlie who looked nothing like the two of them, but looked exactly like Carrie Ann.

Rebecca sat on Ian's right and Travis on his left. Andy and Freddy, Ian's twin son's sat next to Rebecca. Carrie Ann sat next to Travis. Peter was next to Carrie Ann and Charlie next to Peter and last but not least,

Gracie was now, in a basket on the floor between Ian and Rebecca. They kept the basket in the kitchen and would use it until Gracie was big enough for the high chair Ian built her.

Travis looked around the table. "You have quite the family."

Ian grinned. "We do, so one or two, when Lois arrives, additional people are always welcome."

Charlie glanced at Travis. What did he think of their family? Did he have family? What was his relationship with Lois?

And, most importantly, why in the world did she care?

CHAPTER TWO

Three days later

Charlie and Travis were side stepping each other. She was doing her best to avoid him.

He was doing his best to always be around her. He even helped her muck the stalls in the barn.

A wagon arrived at the house from Portland carrying all the furniture for Travis' law office and his assistant, Lois Lattimer. He'd sent a wire when he knew they would be staying with Ian. He hadn't found an office yet but had made arrangements to keep the wagon until he was able to unload it into an office.

Lois was beautiful, with shining black hair and the greenest eyes Charlie had ever seen. Any red-blooded American male would be interested in her. She was dressed in a dark green velvet traveling suit that almost matched her eyes. In short if Charlie had been a girly girl, she'd want to be Lois Lattimer.

Travis walked up to the wagon and helped his assistant down.

She hugged him and kissed his cheek.

"Travis. I'm so glad to finally be here. Jack was so wonderful, telling me about this country and generally keeping me entertained the whole way from Portland."

Walking over to the driver, Travis extended his hand. "Thanks so much for taking care of her, Jack."

"My pleasure, Mr. MacGregor. Miss Lattimer was a joy to travel with."

Charlie couldn't tell if the driver meant it or if he was just angling for a better tip. If it had been her she would be after the better tip. Something about Lois made her skin crawl. She didn't like nor trust the woman. Perhaps because she wanted to treat the woman to a good licking. *Stop it Charlie*, she admonished herself. *What in the world is the matter with you?*

December 12, 1854

Travis buttoned up the sheepskin coat. He'd purchased it a week ago on his second day in Oregon City. All of the Taylor's and the Stanton's had them and he figured there was probably a good reason.

As soon as he put it on, he was warm for the first time since landing in Portland on December 1ˢᵗ, nearly a week before. Now he followed Charlie out to do her chores.

"What do you do first? I'll help."

Charlie looked at him with at eyebrow raised. "Do you know how to milk a cow? We have three to milk now. While on the wagon train we only had one, but we've purchased a couple of more since then. We can't use all the milk so we sell it to the mercantile."

"You didn't come by ship then? It is an easier trip than across on a wagon train."

"It is if you don't get sea sick and don't have livestock to bring with you. We had the cows, chickens, horses and the oxen. The trip on a ship including all of those animals would have been outrageously expensive."

He nodded. "I suppose that's true. You can teach me to milk a cow. Then I can help you every morning."

"Why would you want to do that?"

"So I can be with you and get to know you better. I like you, Charlie."

"I think you're crazy."

———

January 21, 1855

. . .

"Tell me more about your travels here. About being on the wagon train," said Travis as they walked to the barn.

"Why would you want to know about that? It was a long arduous journey."

"Did you wear your pants and guns on the trip?"

"Of course, I did. I even used them to hunt rabbits with. The pistols are not powerful enough to bring down a deer or elk."

She picked up a milk stool and went to one of the black and white cows. "If you want to learn get that milk stool." She jutted her chin toward the stools sitting by the wall.

He got the stool and set it next to her.

Charlie used the wet towel she brought to clean the udder and teats before she started to milk the animal.

Travis sat on the stool he brought. "Why are the milk cows different than the other cows?"

She took hold of one of the teats and pulled and squeezed. The milk began to flow and she squirted it on the ground. "They are a different kind of animal. They are Holsteins. Most beef cattle are Herefords." A dozen cats and kittens came running as soon as she sat down. Now, they were lapping up the milk on the ground.

"And why are you squirting the milk on the ground? To feed the cats?"

"To get the old milk out of the teat." She turned the teat and squirted a couple of the cats and one kitten. "We only want the good fresh milk. Now, you'll take a teat in each hand like this, then you pull and squeeze, pull and squeeze. Soon you'll have milk flowing, from Elsie."

"Is that my cow's name? What are the other cows named?"

"Bessie and Bob."

Travis raised his eyebrows. "Bob?"

Charlie laughed. "That was the cow we brought with us. Carrie Ann named her when she was about two and a half. She named her Bob and it stuck."

"So, are you going to try milking her or just sit there with her teats in your hands?"

"Milking." He squeezed and pulled and pulled and squeezed, all to no avail."

"Here let me help you." Charlie knelt beside him and put her hands over his. "Okay, now pull and squeeze. That's right. You'll get to the point where you do them almost at the same time. Try again. Pull and squeeze. Good." She let go of his hands and he felt bereft. He liked the feel of her hands on his. But he did as she showed him and soon he was squirted the milk on the ground and tried squirting a cat but got Charlie's boot instead.

"I'm sorry. I guess my aim is off."

She shrugged. "These boots have seen much worse. You continue here. You can start putting the milk in the bucket."

He milked the cow until the bucket was almost full. "What do I do if there is more milk than one bucket? Start a new bucket or leave the milk?"

"You can put it in this bucket. That's my overage. I'll go milk Bob now. You can take the two full buckets to the house and put them on the counter by the sink. And Travis,"

"Yes?"

"Thanks. You made my chore more enjoyable."

He smiled. "You're very welcome. I enjoyed learning something new and look forward to helping you again."

"Whenever you like."

February 6, 1855

Together in the barn, Travis and Ian, forked clean straw into the newly mucked stalls. When they were done with the straw, they placed a flake of hay in each feed trough.

"The Valentine's Day dance is coming up," said Ian. "Are you taking anyone?"

"If you mean are Lois and I going together, the answer is no. Ben asked her and she accepted. Thank, God."

"You sound a bit overjoyed."

"I am. I didn't want to take her but was afraid I would have to."

"Well, who do you want to take?"

"Charlie."

"So ask her."

Travis grimaced and shook his head. "It's not that easy. Charlie...she's special." *She's more than special. I could actually consider courting her and marrying her. She makes me feel things I've never felt before.*

Ian lifted an eyebrow. "You are completely mesmerized by my little sister-in-law, aren't you?"

Travis' shoulders dropped and he sighed. "I am. I want to get to know her more than anything but she avoids me at every turn. I have however learned how to muck stalls, milk cows, feed chickens and gather eggs by following her in the mornings.

"I feel like an idiot, considering we all live together in the same house. Which reminds me, I must look for a home of my own or at least a place for Lois. I don't like the fact of having to live with her and work with her, even with a lot of other people around, it's too much. But I've been looking and haven't found anything suitable. The ones I like are too expensive and the ones that are in the price range I want for her are not very nice."

"So you and Lois aren't courting?"

"Good Lord, no. Though I know she would like to be. Heck Ian, I never wanted an assistant, I simply couldn't figure out a way to get rid of her. She kept showing up every day and working anyway. She'd help me with my overflow clients, as I was doing fairly well. I needed the help, so I made her an offer to be my assistant."

Ian leaned on the rake in his hands. "I'm sorry to

hear the problems you've had. Travis, you have to tell her she is only your business assistant...nothing more and definitely not anything personal. You will not be lovers. If you don't tell her she'll always think you are more than business associates."

Travis clinched his jaw and fisted his hands. "I did tell her the first time she made overtures to me. She is well aware nothing more is between us. But I don't think she believes me, especially since she moved here with me. But I don't want to marry and have children. I'm afraid I'll be like my father who never wanted me or had time for me. I don't want to be like that."

Ian clasped a hand on his shoulder. "I'm sure you won't be like your father. If you marry it will be because you want to."

"I hope you're right. I don't want to make the same mistakes he did."

Ian patted his shoulder and then removed his hand. "Don't worry. Now, you moved the business. She had the opportunity then not to come but she chose to follow you here. And since she is aware no personal relationship exists between the two of you, her move is not your fault."

A tightness resided in his chest. "It feels like it's my responsibility even though I know it isn't. Anyway getting her out of your house is another reason for me to find a house. I'll be looking for her to have one of her own, too."

"A few of the houses on Main Street are available

and I even know of a building where you could house your office, unless you were planning on working out of your home like you do here."

"Actually, since Lois will be working there, too, I'd rather not work from the house."

"Understood. Well, come with me and we'll see what we can find."

"I'm following you."

———

At about two-thirty in the afternoon, Charlie sat at the kitchen table cleaning her gun.

Lois entered the kitchen and sat across from her.

"Charlotte, may I have a word with you?"

Charlie didn't look up. She'd been trying to avoid Lois. She didn't like the woman and didn't like the fact she was going to the dance with Ben, but there was nothing she could do about that. She knew her brother well enough to know he would only dig his heels in rather than admit Charlie might be right. "Not as long as you're insisting on calling me Charlotte."

"Oh, very well. Charlie, may I have a word with you?"

She set down her pistol and looked up with a smile. "Certainly. What can I do for you?"

"I want you to know, I'm marrying Travis."

"Oh really. Does he know this?" *Why is she telling me this? I haven't shown any interest in Travis, though we have been spending more time together since he decided to help me with my chores in the morning. I have to admit, the man is growing on me. He's funny and kind but he's still a man.*

Lois looked down at the table. "Well, he might not have gotten the hint yet, but he must mean to, he brought me here didn't he?"

"You followed him here, that's all. Your being here is no fault of his. You are his assistant and according to him that's all you are. Is he wrong?"

Lois waved her hand in a dismissive gesture. "He's just being hard-headed that's all. He thinks I'm just his assistant when I can assure you we are ever so much more to each other. In other words, stay away from Travis."

Charlie gazed at her, not believing a word she said. "That is my intention. Now if you'll excuse me, I have to finish this and see if I can shoot something for dinner."

She wrinkled her nose and her mouth turned down. "Eww, you shoot your dinner?"

She crossed her arms and smiled. "You haven't minded for the last few weeks you've been here."

Lois raised a hand to her throat. "I didn't know. How awful."

Charlie shrugged. "Don't eat it, suit yourself. Just more for everyone else."

"Humpft." Lois left, her skirt swirling around her feet.

Charlie laughed. *That woman is a nitwit. I don't understand what Travis sees in her. Oh well, not my business.*

"That was rather rude, wouldn't you say?" asked Rebecca as she entered the kitchen from the hall to the foyer.

Charlie started a little and then turned to look at her sister. "I thought so, too, but I can't control what comes out of that woman's mouth."

Rebecca stood next to Charlie and put her hands on her hips. "I meant you. That outlandish story about shooting our dinner. Where do you shoot it? At the butcher's? Really, Charlie, that's just..." she began to chuckle. "Ridiculous." She laughed outright.

Charlie joined her sister's laughter.

Rebecca sat across from her. "She might be an idiot but you shouldn't encourage her."

"I can't help myself. But I'll try to be a better hostess."

"Thank you."

"I said I'd try...not that I would succeed." Charlie grinned.

An hour or so later, Charlie grabbed her hat off a peg in the kitchen and headed to the front door. She thought she'd take Gulliver out for a ride before dinner.

As she opened the door she heard footsteps rushing down the stairs.

"Charlie, may I speak with you?"

She turned to face Travis, whose voice she recognized. "Sure what can I do for you?"

He walked up to her and took her hands in his. "I want to take you to the Valentine's Day dance on Saturday, the 10th."

"I know what date Saturday is." She raised an eyebrow and crossed her arms over her ample chest. "Why do you want to take me? What about Lois?" Her heart beat faster and her pulse raced. *Do I really want to go with him? Unfortunately, the answer is yes, I do, much to my annoyance.*

"Ben is taking Lois...but...er...I wouldn't have taken her anyway. She's only my assistant, nothing more."

"Better tell her because I don't think she's convinced of that fact."

Travis frowned. "What do you mean?"

"I mean she warned me off of you just a couple of hours ago. Told me she intends to marry you that you just haven't gotten the message yet, but I better stay away. So consider me...away." She adjusted her hat and tightened the string ties holding it on and went out the door.

Travis followed her. "Wait, Charlie. Please."

She turned and faced him. "What?"

His eyebrows were raised and he did look sincere. "I want you to go to the Valentine's Dance with me. Please."

"Why me?"

"Because I like you. I want to know you better."

Charlie looked at him for a moment. He was a handsome man and he was nice, at least so far. She'd make an enemy of Lois if she went, she knew that. And she hadn't danced in years but she did remember how. She'd watched Rebecca and Ian on numerous occasions.

"All right. I'll go with you. See you downstairs at six on Saturday."

Travis smiled wide. "Thank you." He lifted her hand and kissed the top. "You won't regret it. We'll have a good time, you'll see."

He walked back inside whistling.

Charlie needed to talk to Rebecca, riding Gulliver could wait. She entered the kitchen. Rebecca stood at the sink. When Charlie got close she saw her sister was peeling potatoes.

"Do you want some help?"

"No, I'm almost done. How can I help you, dear sister?"

Charlie leaned back against the counter her hands on either side of her. "I decided to go to the dance with Travis."

"I thought you weren't about to do that. What changed your mind?"

"I'm not letting Lois or anyone else tell me who I can talk to, or see, or be friends with. So, I'm going to the dance, but I don't have any dresses."

"I still have your Sunday dress from seven years ago, before you started wearing pants. You should still be able to wear it. If not then we'll see if you can wear mine."

"I should have known you would keep something. Thank you. My body has changed and I only have boots to wear, so we'll see how it fits."

Rebecca cut the last potato into the large pot of water, then set the pot on the stove and wiped her hands with a towel. "Let's go see what we have to work with."

She placed her arm through Charlie's and they walked arm-in-arm up the stairs.

When Charlie and Rebecca reached her bedroom, she went in and directly to the cedar chest at the foot of the bed. Rebecca rummaged around in it until she found the dress.

Charlie remembered the garment. It was a dark blue serge with white cuffs and collar. It buttoned up the front and was very winkled.

"Let me shut the door and you can try it on," said Rebecca.

When the door was shut Charlie stripped down to her bloomers and chemise. She put on the dress and buttoned it up. The buttons strained over her chest, but it didn't look bad and it had been her favorite dress. The length was a little short with her boots on but she didn't figure anyone would notice because they would be dancing.

She closed her eyes. This was a bad idea. She should never have agreed to go but she didn't have any choice now. Charlie refused to back out. When she said she'd do something she was giving her word. And her word was her bond.

Saturday, February 10th

She patted her hair. Rebecca had twisted it into a French chignon. It looked nice she thought. She pinched her cheeks and bit her lips bringing color to both of them.

Charlie went downstairs at five minutes until six and found Travis already in the foyer. He looked very handsome in his black suit with matching vest. He wore a white shirt and black bow tie and held a stovepipe hat in his hand.

He took her hand and kissed the top. "You look beautiful. Can I help you with your coat?"

"Sure. Let me get it." She went to the coat closet and returned with her sheepskin coat.

He took the garment and helped her into it.

"Thank you. You don't have to compliment me. I don't expect it."

"I'm saying you're beautiful because you are. It's a statement of fact. I'm a lawyer remember? I deal in facts." He slipped on his dress coat. The same one he was wearing the first time they met.

She laughed. "You're different than any lawyer I've ever heard of, though you're the first one I've met in person. I will also admit you look rather dashing yourself."

He put his hand over the top of hers as they began walking to the community hall for the dance. "Good, I don't want to be like every other attorney. I want to be the best."

Charlie looked at him. "I believe you will be."

"Thank you."

"Rebecca is bringing our food contribution. She and Ian will be coming in the buggy since they were bringing Gracie and the other kids, as well as the food."

"Good. I believe that Ben and Lois have already left for the dance."

They heard the music and saw people dancing as they approached the community hall. Inside lanterns were on the walls every few feet so it was brightly lit.

"Would you care to dance, m'lady?" Travis released her arm and gave her a bow.

Charlotte frowned. "Do you have to call more attention to us than necessary? Everyone is already looking at us. I'm sure some of them would be very happy to see me fall flat on my face."

He smiled. "I think they are looking at us because they've never seen such a beautiful woman before."

He knew just what to say to get her smiling or rolling her eyes or in this case both.

"You're crazy. They've never seen me in a dress before that's all."

"You can see what you want, but I see the truth."

Lois came up to them. She was wearing a green silk dress with a low neckline and fitted bodice. It fit her absolutely perfectly. The garment had obviously been made just for her. Her hair shone in black curls gathered at her nape.

Ben, in his Sunday suit, followed carrying two glasses of punch.

"Well, I see you made it." Lois looked Charlie up and down. "You know," she said loudly, "you really should lengthen your dresses if you insist on wearing those hideous boots."

Everyone around them stopped and stared at Charlie. Her stomach clenched and her hands formed fists. *I shouldn't care what these people...any of them think of me. But I do. I admit, I want to be liked and I want to have friends, but I never will if they keep thinking of me the way Lois wants them to.*

"You should learn to keep your opinions to yourself." Charlie turned and left the building, walking, head held high, until she cleared the area in view of the community center. Then she broke into a run and didn't stop until she reached home.

CHAPTER THREE

"Charlie. Charlie wait," Travis called.

She ignored him, lifted her skirt and ran home. Once home, she flung open the door and pounded up the stairs, unbuttoning the hated dress as she went. When she reached her bedroom she slammed the door shut, ripped her arms out of the dress and let it drop to the floor. Then she removed her boots and put on her regular clothes, including her gun belt, before donning her boots once again. Then she took her hair out of the bun Rebecca had fashioned and let it hang loose to her waist.

When she was done dressing she wadded up the dress, took it to Rebecca's room and dropped it at the door.

"Feel better?" Travis stood on the landing at the top of the stairs, leaning against the stair railing with his arms crossed over his chest.

"As a matter of fact I do. I never should have tried to be someone I'm not."

He walked over to her. "How long have you been wearing pants? Months, years? How long?"

Charlie pushed her hair behind her ears. "About seven years, since just before Carrie Ann was born. Why?"

He tucked a strand she missed behind her ear. "You haven't forgotten how to wear a dress, you were just embarrassed because you don't have the proper shoes any longer. Lois was quite wrong in pointing that out in public."

"Lois is a witch, with a "b", and I don't mean a female dog."

He ran a hand behind his neck. "Yes, she is. I'm afraid she sees you as a threat. She's afraid that I'll be interested in courting you."

"She's crazy."

He didn't say anything.

She cocked her head to one side and narrowed her eyes. "She is crazy, isn't she?"

Taking her hands in his, he smiled. "No. She's not crazy. I very much want to court you. I want to marry you Charlie and courting is the way that needs to proceed."

She pulled back her hands. "You've lost your mind, too. You don't even know me."

"That's the reason for the courtship, to get to know each other better."

Charlie worried the inside of her cheek with her teeth. "I don't know."

His lips formed a small smile. "Come on. Give me... give us a chance."

She found herself wavering. Despite all her misgivings about men, Charlie really did like Travis. He was everything she'd wanted in a man before her father broke her trust. So why was she being stubborn about this?

"Tell you what. Go fishing with me tomorrow and I'll give you my answer when we return home."

"Deal." He took one of her hands again and kissed the top.

Charlie took a deep breath and then let it out again. "I still think you're a crazy man."

Travis threw back his head and laughed before leaning forward and placing a kiss on her cheek. "Until later."

She nodded. "I'll be sitting on the porch with a glass of tea. Would you like to join me?"

I want to touch my cheek where he kissed me, but he'd just see it as rubbing it in. Is that what I'd be doing? I've never met anyone like Travis and he is nicer than any man I've met before. Should I take a chance? Will I lose the only opportunity for a family if I don't accept his courting? No, that's not why I want him to court me, why I'll say yes tomorrow. I'm captivated by Travis MacGregor, Esquire. I may even be falling in love.

"Sure. Anything to spend more time with you."

Charlie shook her head and rolled her eyes.

She brought out the pitcher of tea and two glasses, setting one glass on the table in front of him.

"So, Travis, how in the world did you get involved with a woman like Lois? Don't get me wrong, she's beautiful. Ben's totally infatuated with her."

"I've told him about Lois and that he should stay away from her but I don't think he believed me. She's trouble. I wish she'd done what I hoped and stayed back in Philadelphia. I never expected her to move out here with me."

"She said you moved her out here with you."

He waved the comment away. "That's not true. I had my passage and all my furniture loaded on the ship when she came up the gang plank and acted like we were long lost lovers. I told her to get away from me and keep away from me."

Charlie lifted an eyebrow. "And did she?"

He sighed. "No. And I admit, we did keep each other company on the ship sometimes. But there were lots of people on the boat with which to converse, so I wasn't stuck with Lois very often."

"You're being obtuse in not recognizing her actions for what they are. She's in love with you and will do anything for you. Tonight she attacked me because she perceives me as a threat." *I watched Ben and Emily go through some of this only it was Ben who was jealous, and as it turned out, with cause since she jilted him. But the situation was definitely a learning experience for Ben and for me. At least I know what to look for in a woman or man obsessed. And Lois is definitely obsessed with Travis.*

"You can't be a threat, since no her and me exists, never has and never will."

Charlie lifted her hands shoulder high and poked herself in the chest. "I'm not the one you have to convince."

"I'll straighten it out. No more incidents like tonight will happen."

"You're right there won't be, because I don't intend to attend any more dances."

He smiled. "But Charlie, it's a good way to meet your neighbors."

She shrugged. "I don't care if I meet the neighbors. The ones I want to know, I already do and the rest can go to...elsewhere."

"Well, I need your help and I need to meet these people. Let them get to know me. You can help with that and if you'd let me court you, we could spend just that much more time together getting to know each other."

Charlie shook her head slowly. "You don't give up do you?"

He grinned. "Not when it comes to you."

"After the fishing trip tomorrow you'll know my answer. Do you have anything other than fancy clothes?" She waved her hand up and down in front of him.

He looked down at his suit. "I'm dressed for a dance. What do you expect me to be wearing?"

"True. But even the everyday clothes I've seen you in aren't appropriate for fishing. See if you can borrow some pants and a shirt from Ian. You're about the same size, though you're a little taller so the pants will be a little short, but you may end up folding them up anyway."

"All right. What else do I have to know about fishing?"

"Well, you need to get up early and then dig worms for bait." She kept her gaze on him, checking his reaction.

His mouth turned down. "That's disgusting."

Charlie laughed. "I knew you'd say that. I guess we can just call the whole thing off—"

"No." He lifted his palm to her. "We're going. What time do you want me up?"

"I'm getting up at four-thirty. I'll meet you in the kitchen at five, that should give you enough time to dress and for me to make breakfast and lunch. Then we'll go outside and dig for worms. How's that sound?"

He frowned and then smiled. "Terrific. I can't wait."

She laughed. If he showed up she'd be surprised. But if he did she'd take him to her favorite spot over by Portland. It was a good three hour ride, but they would still get there in plenty of time for some of the best fishing.

Charlie was just finishing the sandwiches for lunch when Travis entered the kitchen. She looked over at him. "Ian's clothes are a little small. I figured it would be the other way around since he does so much physical labor and you...well, you don't."

He came to stand beside her at the counter. "You might be surprised at what I do for fun."

"Oh? And what is that?"

"I participate in the Highland Games and the caber toss."

Charlie's mouth fell open. She couldn't help it. Never in a million years would she have suspected he participated in something like those Scottish games. "Well, I must say I'm impressed, but I wouldn't wear your kilt to go fishing."

Travis grinned. "I hadn't planned on it, though if I'd known what your reaction would be, I might have considered it. How do you know about the games?"

She ignored his quip. "I knew a Scottish girl back in Independence and she took me to the games. I think she was trying to get me interested in her brother, who also tossed the caber."

"Most interesting. I'm finding out more and more about you, Charlie Taylor."

"Well, I've got breakfast and lunch." She packed it all in her saddlebags. "You don't mind sandwiches do you. I have fried egg sandwiches for breakfast and roast beef for lunch. I made plenty so we shouldn't go hungry and Rebecca baked molasses cookies yesterday for the dance. Luckily she also left some here for us, so I have a few of those."

"You seem to have thought of everything." Picking up a lantern, he held open the door to the backyard. "Shall we?"

"We shall." She walked through and stopped about ten feet from the door. Then she pointed toward the house. "There's a shovel leaning up against the side of the house. Grab it please."

He took the shovel in his free hand.

She walked over to a large oval metal bath tub. "Okay turn the dirt over. Gently, please."

He turned the dirt by shovelfuls. In the lantern light squirmed the slimy bodies of large earthworms.

Charlie grabbed a small bucket sitting by the bathtub. She put several handfuls of dirt into the bucket and then plucked worms one at a time and dropped them in.

"You'll find a little bucket on that side, too. Do what I did and start gathering worms."

"How do you grow them in this tub?"

"Worms split in order to reproduce. We feed them coffee grounds, egg shells and such and they multiply so we always have a supply."

"That's a great idea."

"We think so. Of course, so did the old man in Independence, Missouri who told us about this method."

"Okay, we've plenty now so let's get the horses."

They headed to the barn and saddled the horses. Charlie tied the fishing gear to their saddles before they mounted up and headed out into the dawn. The slight breeze was enough to make her happy they were both wearing their sheepskin coats.

"Are you hungry?" Charlie asked. "We can eat now or wait a while. We're going to my favorite place and it's about three hours away, north and west of here."

"I am hungry, but our hands are filthy."

"It's just a little good honest dirt and won't hurt you. Here." She handed him a fried egg sandwich made with butter, mayonnaise and mustard. "Besides it's wrapped in waxed paper which will protect the sandwich from the dirt."

He took the sandwich and watched her eat before opening his and taking a bite.

"See? No dirt and if you do get some on your sandwich, dirt doesn't hurt you. Besides, you barely have any on your fingers."

Travis looked at his hands and shrugged. "I guess I'll have to get used to getting a little dirty if I'm going to court you."

She laughed. "Court me? You take a lot for granted Mr. MacGregor. But we'll see, and if I agree, you'll have to take me as I am because I don't intend to change. You saw what happened when I tried to be someone I'm not anymore."

"See you said *anymore*, so you did used to dress like a girl."

Even the call of the robins and the meadowlarks didn't ease her pain. She still felt the anger and hatred of her father, even though he was gone for many years. "Of course, I did, until my father kicked me out of the house. Then I started wearing pants so I could find work. I returned home after he died."

"I didn't know. I wondered what happened that changed you. Having your father kick you out would do that."

She turned in her saddle and looked at him. "Don't feel sorry for me. I don't and I don't want others to. I'm who I am because of my father, the good and the bad. Let's leave it at that."

He frowned. "I don't...feel sorry for you, I mean. I admire you. You were faced with adversity and overcame it. That's amazing."

"Hmpft. Amazing for a woman, you mean."

"No, for anyone the age you were then, you're young?"

"I was just seventeen."

"What did you find a job doing?"

"The feed store hired me to load wagons."

He lifted a brow. "That's a hard job...for anyone."

"You're right it was hard, but it prepared me to be able to do anything I think I can. Stop." She pulled Gulliver to a halt. "Look to your left over there in the trees, see her?"

"No, what?"

"A doe. She's standing still hoping we don't see her,

but I do and if I was hunting she would be mine. But I only hunt when we need the food. Some people come from Portland and hunt for trophies. They leave the animal to rot and take just the bugle teeth or the horns. At least it feeds the other predators for a while."

After they'd passed the Oregon City wayfarer's cabin and then had been on the road for about two hours, they passed the wayfarers shack on the Portland side, when she turned off to the right and pointed ahead of them. "See this path we'll follow it to a clearing. The stream is through the trees just the other side of the little meadow. We'll hobble the horses there." She dug in her heels and galloped along the path, then walked and then galloped again, just as they'd done on the journey along the road.

When they reached the clearing, she galloped across it, letting Gulliver have his head.

Travis followed at a slower pace.

Catching her Appaloosa stallion was difficult on the best of days, but now after riding for almost three hours, his poor rented horse didn't have a chance.

"Whoa, boy. That's a good boy."

She was off her horse and unpacking when he arrived.

"Do you ever slow down?"

"What for? Time for fishing is the very best now until about twelve or one. So shake a leg and let's go, we've only got about four hours."

Travis slid from the saddle and unloaded his fishing gear and worms.

She walked a short ways to the rushing water.

He followed.

Charlie pointed at a spot downstream. "You see that big rock in the middle?"

"Yes."

"On the other side is a deep hole. That's where the best fish are."

"How do we get there?"

"I'll show you."

She unpacked her pole and put it together including the reel, strung it with fishing line, put weights and a hook on and then the worm.

She watched as Travis did the same. Much to her surprise he seemed to know what he was doing.

"You've done this before, haven't you?"

He grinned. "Just a few times, with Ian. This is my first time with worms, though."

She lifted an eyebrow, not knowing whether to believe him or not.

"Well since you've been before you should know how to float the bait down the stream into the hole, right?"

"Yes, I can manage."

They'd been fishing for about twenty minutes when Charlie's line went slack. She carefully tightened it until she felt the bite, then she quickly brought up the pole and set the hook before reeling the fish in. It was a nice fourteen-inch brook trout.

Fishing until about eleven o'clock they'd both done well. Charlie caught eight fish and Travis landed seven.

Clouds quickly formed and she knew they needed to get away from the water and find shelter.

"Travis, we're about to get drenched." She pointed at the clouds, which had turned nearly black. "Take apart your equipment and pack up. We might make it to the wayfarer's shack before the rain starts."

She packed quickly and then rode at a gallop.

Travis galloped behind her.

But the heavens opened and they were drenched by the time they reached the shack.

"Go inside and start a fire. I'll take the horses to the lean-to," shouted Charlie over the sound of the rain, claps of thunder and even worse...lightning.

"Okay. Hurry."

She led the horses and then took off their saddles and put them on the rail for that purpose on the inside of the lean-to. Then she grabbed the saddle bags and ran to the cabin.

"Oh, thank God you have that fire going." She stood in front of it and rubbed her hands together. Then she went to the box in the corner and pulled out two blankets.

Travis took the blanket from her and held it up. "These will help, but we have to get out of these wet clothes if we want to get dry and keep from getting sick."

She shook her head. "I ca...ca...can't do that." *I can't get naked in front of him. I may be different in the way I act, but I'm still a woman and I can't do it.*

"Listen to you. Your teeth are chattering. I'll turn my back and we can both get undressed and wrap in the blankets."

"Bu...bu..but," *How can I do this? It's wrong. But so is catching my death because I am too stubborn to be logical.*

"Charlie, no one will know. We'll dress again before we go home and our clothes will be mostly dry."

"I guess you're ri...r...right." *He's right. No one will know. We'll be home before dark, dry and all will be well, including me.*

"You know I'm right."

She closed her eyes for a moment and then nodded.

Travis turned his back.

She turned hers, doffed all her wet clothes and laid them on the floor in front of the fire to dry.

"Do we still have sandwiches?" asked Travis, wrapped in a blanket tucked under his arms much as hers was. "I could use one right about now."

Relieved at the change in topic, she said, "We do. We still have a fried egg sandwich each and two roasted beef each plus molasses cookies."

"Too bad we don't have coffee to go with it."

She grinned. "Ask and ye shall receive." Clutching the

blanket around her she walked over to the kitchen area of the cabin. There was a bucket, a coffee pot and several shelves above the counter with a single container on them and four coffee cups. "Coffee and water are always kept here and at the wayfarer's cabin by Oregon City. The Portland marshal takes care of this place and Robert McCauley, our marshal, takes care of the cabin by our home."

Dipping water from the bucket into the coffee pot, she rinsed the pot of any insects and clumsily threw the water outside as she clutched the blanket to her. Then she made a pot of coffee. Since the cups were upside down she didn't need to rinse them.

While the coffee boiled, Charlie tried to dry her hair in front of the fire and hold up the blanket. It was difficult to do, but by the time the coffee was done, about thirty minutes after she started, her hair was about half dry. The coffee was good and strong and she poured them each a cup. They sat at the small table and she again had a difficult time eating and trying to hold up her blanket.

They ate sandwiches, cookies and drank hot coffee which did more to warm them up than the fire.

Charlie found a deck of cards in her saddlebags and they played for hours while the clothes dried. They played poker with matchsticks.

She dealt the next hand of draw poker. "So, Ian told Rebecca that you found a house. When will you move in?"

"It won't be ready until next Thursday. I'll take three

cards." He threw down three from his hand and picked up the three she dealt to him.

"You'll enjoy having your own home. Lots more privacy for one thing. Dealer takes two." She threw down two cards and dealt herself two more. "What do you bet?"

"Four matches."

She laughed. "I'll see your four and raise you four."

"Aha." He grinned. "You fell right into my trap. Read 'em and weep, my lovely."

He laid three tens, a jack and an ace on the table.

"You lose." She laid down her hand. "Let the cards speak for themselves."

"You have three kings and that's all you bet?" His voice rose on 'bet'.

"I got your money, didn't I?"

He nodded. "Touché.

Finally, about four hours after they arrived, the clothes on the floor were dry.

"Shall we get dressed? We'll do it just like we did when we undressed." She turned her back and trusted him to do the same. Then she dressed. Her clothes were warm from the fire and felt wonderful. Her hair was dry, though it seemed to take forever for the thick, blonde mass to do so.

At about six hours since they arrived, Travis finally commented. "The rain doesn't appear to be stopping."

"Nope but it's not the rain that bothers me. If it was just raining we could have ridden in it. It's the lightning.

And if it strikes anywhere near the cabin, there could be a forest fire and that could be very dangerous. But even more worrisome, if we leave, we're without protection from that lightning and could easily be struck."

"You know what it means if we have to stay here all night. We could try riding home, rain or not."

She took a deep breath. "Not in this lightning. And yes, I realize the ramifications if we stay here all night. But they can't make us marry. I don't care what people think about me."

"Well you may not, but I care what they think about me. I have a law practice to begin here and can't have it start by tarnishing your name and mine. We'll have to marry when we get back."

She started to chew a nail. "And I suppose that pleases you no end."

"No, actually it doesn't. I wanted you to marry me because you wanted to, not because you have to."

"Well, that doesn't appear to be happening and since we're getting married anyway, I don't see any point in not sleeping together. After our early morning, I'm tired."

"Me, too."

Charlie went to the bed, removed her boots and guns, laid down and covered herself with the blanket. *I know this is the last night I'll be without a husband. I know we'll have to marry when we get home, but I wish it wasn't so. I really wanted to get to know him before we married.*

Travis widened his eyes and he shook his head. "You

can't mean we sleep together. Charlie, think what that means."

"I know what it means and figure we might as well get used to sleeping together since we will be from now on." She turned back the blanket and patted the bed. "You can get into the bed. Spread your blanket on top of us for warmth."

"Are you sure?"

She opened her eyes. "Will you please get into bed, I'm already cold."

"Okay. I'm coming."

He climbed into bed. "I'm sorry, Charlie. I really didn't want this."

"I know. We have no control over the weather, so maybe God is telling me that you're the one I'm supposed to marry."

"Perhaps."

"I'm still cold. Will you hold me?" She felt the heat from his body as he scooted closer.

"With pleasure. After we're married, I hope you'll let me hold you like this every night."

"We'll see. We might as well get some sleep. Morning will be here soon enough and so will the consequence of this night."

My life will totally change now. If it was just me, I wouldn't care, but I can't destroy Travis' reputation before he even really gets started in business. Will he expect me to host dinner parties and such? Can I be the wife of a lawyer?

CHAPTER FOUR

After having the last two roast beef sandwiches for breakfast, Travis cleaned the coffee pot while Charlie filled the water bucket.

"Are you ready to go?" She placed her hands on her hips.

"Yes. Let's get the horses."

They walked in silence to the lean-to, saddled the horses and headed home.

Arriving more than two hours later, they took care of their mounts before going inside.

The questions will start and I don't know what to say. That this situation is all my fault? That I knew better than to take him so far away? Yes, to all that. I knew better, but I was being my stubborn self. Sure if I rode him hard enough, he'd give up wanting to court me. Looks like my plan ricocheted on me.

In the kitchen, Rebecca turned from the sink where

she was doing the dishes. "Where have you been? You were gone all night."

Charlie shrugged. "The rain chased us into the wayfarer's cabin by Portland and we were soaked as it was. Then the rain never let up, and the lightning was unbelievable, so we stayed in the cabin all night. We are fully aware of what we need to do now, so we'll go see Reverend Trowbridge after we clean up."

Rebecca dried her hands before putting her arms around her sister. "I'm sorry, Charlie. This is not what I wanted for you."

"I know, but it doesn't matter. Travis wanted to court me and I was about to give him my answer after we were done fishing."

"You never did give me your answer," said Travis.

She gave Rebecca a final squeeze and went to Travis. She kissed him on the cheek. "I was going to say, yes. I guess that's why I'm not so upset about the result of our night in the shack."

He put his arms around her. "I'm so glad." He lowered his lips and caught hers in a gentle kiss.

Wrapping her arms around his neck, she returned his kiss.

He pulled back. "I'll do my best to make you happy."

She cupped his jaw with a hand. "I know you will and I'll do the same, but don't expect me to change. If you need a prissy wife to court your clients, you should pick someone else."

"We'll work it out."

She narrowed her eyes. "I don't think you realize that I mean what I say. I won't change how I am, pants and all."

Rebecca agreed. "She means it, Travis. She is not the wife for you if you want someone to coddle your clients."

Travis smiled at her. "I accept you...just as you are. I promise."

"Good." Charlie turned to Rebecca. "Can you and Ian stand up with us? Come with us, to see Reverend Trowbridge, now before the gossips have too much time to make things up? We should probably get Ben, Peter and the little kids."

"All right. Let me find Ian," said Rebecca.

"I'll do that," said Travis. "I want to tell him before he gets the chance to punch me."

Rebecca nodded. "Last I saw him he was out front."

"Okay." He turned and went through the door to the front door.

"Are you okay," Rebecca asked Charlie. "I'll get the others while you're getting cleaned up. If you're all right."

Charlie nodded. "I will be. Like I said I was going to let him court me. I thought that would put off a wedding until we knew each other better, but this will just force us to learn quickly.'

"Marriage will do that. You should know that I don't regret my marriage to Ian. I loved him before we married and I love him now even more."

"I'm glad to hear that, wife," said Ian as he entered, Travis behind him. He walked over to Rebecca, wrapped his arms around her and kissed her. "Because I feel the exact same way. If Travis and Charlie are half as lucky as we've been they'll have a happy marriage."

Rebecca leaned into Ian's side. "You do know what to say to make me happy."

Charlie rolled her eyes. "Okay you two, we get the idea."

"I've already told her I'd do my best to make her happy and we are already happy. Right, Charlie?" asked Travis.

She narrowed her eyes and frowned at Travis. "I know you're just saying that to reassure Rebecca and Ian, but they don't need the reassurance. So let's go get this over with. I need to change clothes first."

"So do I. Meet you back here in fifteen minutes?"

"That will be fine."

She walked out of the kitchen, followed by Travis.

———

I never should have let this happen. I knew it was supposed to rain. It always does, but I never expected the deluge that we got. I should have. I shouldn't have taken him so far away from home. What in the world was I thinking? And now? I'm getting married. I never thought I'd be married...not after I started wearing pants and carrying pistols.

———

Ian drove the wagon down to the Trowbridge home. It was the only conveyance they had that would carry everyone. Since it was Monday, the reverend would probably be at the house.

When they stopped, Charlie jumped down and held her arms up for Gracie. She was five-and-a-half months old and more fun to be with. Charlie could do things with her, play with her now, that she couldn't do before. Charlie flew her around in a circle.

Gracie giggled.

The sound of a baby's giggle always made everything all right. It had to because nothing about this situation was all right. Charlie had never been more miserable in her life, except when her father threw her out. She'd ruined not only her life but Travis'. He didn't think that way, but Charlie knew better.

Ian came around to help Rebecca down and she then took Gracie from Charlie.

Charlie and Travis led the way up to the Trowbridge home.

Charlie knocked.

The door opened, and Mrs. Trowbridge, a short, round woman with gray hair and a constant smile, stood in the doorway.

"Well, hi there, folks. What can I do for you all?"

"We're looking for the reverend. Is he in?" asked Charlie.

The little woman shook her head. "Oh, my no. He's at the church working on his sermon."

Travis took Charlie's hand. "Thank you. We'll go find him."

The Trowbridge's marriage seemed to be a happy one. Was it only her parents that had an unhappy marriage? So far every one she'd come in contact with had a happy marriage.

Charlie looked down at their clasped hands. "What's this for?" She raised their hands.

Travis smiled. "You seemed a little nervous."

"I'm not nervous."

"Then I guess it was me." He grinned at his joke.

Charlie rolled her eyes but couldn't help a smile and squeezed his hand.

Entering the church they saw Reverend Trowbridge at the lectern.

"Reverend."

"Come in, my children, come in." Reverend Trowbridge waved them forward as he came to meet them..

"Hi reverend," said Charlie. "We've come here to get married...today."

The reverend's eyebrows went up. "Today? Did something happen I should know about?"

Charlie looked down, embarrassed to admit she'd made a mistake. "Travis and I were caught in a rain storm and had to weather the night together in a cabin with no chaperone. Although nothing happened between us, the gossips will never believe that. We know we would have to do this sooner or later, and we'd rather it was sooner. Travis has a business that needs to be above reproach, and while I don't care what others think about me, I do care what they believe about him."

He turned to Travis. "And what about you, young man?"

"I intended to court Charlie with the outcome being marriage, so this hastened ceremony is just pushing up the result of our courting a bit."

"Do you love her?" asked the reverend.

Charlie gazed over at him, more interested in what he said to this question than to any other. *Does he love me?*

Travis shuffled his feet. "In all honesty, I don't know. I know that I like her an awful lot, but whether that is love or not, I don't know."

"Very well. I see you brought your witnesses along."

"Yes, we wanted to make sure the wedding was done today," said Charlie.

The reverend spread his arms wide. "Then shall we proceed?"

"Yes, sir. Thank you," said Travis.

"Charlie and Travis will stand in front of me, Charlie on my right. Rebecca will stand on Charlie's left.. Travis and Ian will do the same on my left."

They all moved to stand where he directed them while he grabbed his Bible from his coat pocket.

"Good. We shall begin. Dearly beloved, we are gathered here in this company and before God to join this man and this woman in holy matrimony. Do you Travis..." He looked up at Travis.

"My middle name is Magus."

Charlie raised her eyebrows. *Magus? His middle name is Magus.*

"Travis Magus MacGregor, take this woman, Charlotte Luanne Taylor, for your lawful wedded wife? To have and to hold, for richer or for poorer, in sickness and in health, and to keep yourself only unto her, from this day forward, as long as you both shall live?"

Travis looked at Charlie. "I do."

"Good. Now, do you, Charlotte Luanne Taylor, take this man, Travis Magus MacGregor, to be your lawful husband? To have and to hold, to honor and obey, for richer or for poorer, in sickness and in health, and to keep yourself only unto him, from this day forward, for as long as you both shall live?"

Charlie's hands shook as she looked into Travis' light green eyes, knowing she'd have said yes when he asked her to marry him, so why did this admission feel so wrong? "I do."

"By the power vested in me by God and the city of Oregon City, I now pronounce you man and wife. You may kiss the bride."

Travis turned to Charlie, lifted her chin with a finger and pressed his lips against hers. He tried to keep the kiss chaste, but she was having none of it and threw her arms around his neck, pressed her body against his and kissed him hard.

She felt his smile and knew they could have a good marriage, whether they ever loved one another or not. They had a great physical attraction and that would have to be enough...for now.

"Hey, you two. Come on now," said Ian.

Rebecca tapped Charlie on the shoulder. "Let's get home. Travis needs to move his things into your bedroom."

Travis loosened the hug and released Charlie. "Her bedroom?"

"Yes, her room is bigger than yours," said Ian.

"Ah. Of course. Luckily I don't have a lot of things to move. And it's only temporary."

"You'll have to tell Lois," said Charlie. "And I think that house you were looking to move into, should be her new home now, don't you?"

"Yes, by all means. I don't want her living at your... our...home any longer than necessary. That house was supposed to be available next Thursday, which would only be five more days including today." He took Charlie's hand in his. "Can you handle her living in the big house a little longer?"

"I can handle it. The bigger question is can she?"

The group arrived back at the house and all the children tumbled out of the wagon and began playing in the front yard. Peter walked the porch stairs, sat and picked up the piece of wood, he was whittling.

Charlie stopped to talk to Peter while the rest of the

adults went inside. "What are you making this time little brother?" She was trying her best not to muss his hair. He was getting too old for that sort of behavior from her.

"A whistle. I'll use it to call in the kids when they are playing, for meals and such."

"That's a good idea. Much better than making them each a whistle. That would drive us all crazy."

"It would and I don't even want to think about the way they would wake the house in the mornings. Listening to them thunder down the stairs is bad enough."

Charlie laughed. "You just stayed up late reading your latest book and then didn't want to get up. The kids are no louder than normal."

He didn't look up. "Maybe."

"No maybe about it. I know you, little brother."

Peter shaved off another sliver of wood. "So you and Travis married now."

Her levity faded. "Yes. We're married."

Peter gazed up at her. "You're not happy about it. Why? He's a good man. You couldn't find one better in Oregon City and I think he likes you."

Charlie looked at Travis who stood with Ian and Rebecca, who held Gracie. They were surrounded by the older three children. "I like him, too." It was the first time she'd admitted it to anyone.

"Then what's the problem?"

She sighed. "You're too young to understand."

"Why is it you, Rebecca and Ben always say that when you don't want to talk about something? I'm not too young to understand you were forced to marry Travis and you don't like that. But if you like him, why would you be upset?"

Charlie ruffled his hair. The reason didn't make enough sense for her to explain. "Like I said, too young." She walked up the porch steps into the house and slipped into the kitchen where she poured a cup of coffee and took a big swig, feeling the burn all the way to her stomach.

"Wishing for something harder in the house?" asked Travis as he entered the room.

"We have whiskey, but given my mood, I'd be drunk in no time at all, and I don't want headache the next day."

Travis took the cup out of her hand and set it on the counter, before taking her into his arms. "We'll be okay. You'll see, just give us a try."

She pulled away. "I don't have any choice now but to *give us a try*. Just because we're sleeping together, doesn't mean we'll make love. I'll get to know who you are before I surrender by body to you."

Charlie walked out of the kitchen and out to the barn. As she walked she wiped the tears away. She wouldn't cry. She wouldn't. What she needed was a good long ride on Gulliver, her Appaloosa stallion. She bridled him and then swung up on his bare back, eschewing a saddle, needing to feel him, his muscle, his strength and let it flow into her.

She left the barn at a gallop passing Travis as he walked out after her.

CHAPTER FIVE

Travis trudged back inside.

As he reached the kitchen door, Ian met him and put a hand on his shoulder. "Don't worry, she'll come around. Give her some time."

"I'm willing to give her the time she needs...but I won't wait forever."

"Do you want an annullment? What would the point of getting married be then?"

"No, I want Charlie for my wife. Have since the first time I saw her, when she charged me to show me the way to Oregon City. And that was in spite of the fact I knew I'd need to marry her. You know how I feel about marriage, but with Charlie, the prospect doesn't seem so awful."

"She charged you?"

"Yup. One dollar and then she went into town, bought a bag of candy and gave it to the local kids. As each child came up, she made sure to tell me their name and what their daddy did for a living. Was she aware of the kind of business I did before I arrived?"

Ian lifted a brow. "She might have been. A big article was in our paper about you and the last company you gutted."

Travis ran a hand through his hair. "I don't do that anymore. I just want a simple quiet life helping people, one person at a time."

"You better make sure she knows that. Her way of introducing you to the children indicates she knew what you did and wanted you to know the actual people you would be hurting."

"Well, I hope my new business will be more to her liking. I don't want my wife to hate me because of what I do."

"You'd better talk to her. Take my horse Pegasus. He's the only one that can possibly keep up with, maybe even catch, Gulliver. He's the big black in the last stall." Ian reached into his pocket and pulled out an apple. "I was taking this to him, now, you can give it to him. He'll like you better."

Travis ran both hands through his hair. "I suppose I better hurry, but what will I say?" *That's rather ironic, me, a man who makes his living with words, having to ask what to say.*

"Just that you used to run a very different business than the one you'll be operating here."

"Yeah. Very different." He ran toward the barn to saddle Pegasus and catch up with Charlie.

———

Charlie galloped along the road toward Portland as fast as Gulliver would go, which, if she thought about it, was very fast. The horse had long legs and a deep chest, so he could run for long distances without slowing. Somehow, he'd run back to the wayfarer's shack that caused her so much trouble.

Inside she realized they hadn't cleaned up the cabin after they used it and so she did it now. She'd been cleaning the cabin for about fifteen minutes when she heard a horse outside.

She looked out the window and saw Travis. He'd followed her on Ian's horse. She threw open the door and crossed her arms over her chest. Charlie was nervous and somewhat excited because he followed her. Did he care? "What do you want? Why'd you follow me? You know, if you'd been on your own horse, you'd never have found me here."

"I know. Ian let me borrow Pegasus, so I could catch you." He swung his arms wide, showing his vulnerability. "Charlie, please listen to me. You need to know I'm not like the person in that article you read."

She turned her back on him and walked away from the door, into the cabin. "The article was about you. I recognized your name. The paper told how you go in and gut businesses, putting people out of work. Is that what you intend to do here?"

He came behind her and turned her to face him. "I don't do that anymore. I want to start fresh. I want to help people even if it means suing the people like the aggressive lawyer I used to be."

"Really?" She looked at him with her eyes narrowed and her chin down.

"Honest." He closed the distance between them and took her in his arms. Lowering his head he placed his lips on hers and kissed her gently. "Do you believe me?"

She nodded. "I believe you." Then she lifted herself on her toes and kissed him deeply and completely.

His eyes widened at her kiss and then closed to concentrate only on her. "I want to make love to you, Charlie."

"I want you to make love to me, too." *I've never said that to anyone else. Having my first time making love occur in a wayfarer's cabin wasn't what I imagined either, but if the time seems right, and now is the time, then the place doesn't matter.*

"Here?"

"Why not? This is where it all started. It seems appropriate that our first time together be here."

"As you wish." He swept her up in his arms, kicked the door shut with his booted foot and carried her to the bed.

Travis let her slide down his body as he set her on the floor. "Do you feel how much I want you?"

Her heart beat fast. "Yes. I want you, too."

He pushed a strand of hair behind her ear. "Are you frightened? I'll do my best not to hurt you and to tell you what is happening?"

She looked up at him and gave him a tremulous smile. "I know what will happen, I was raised on a farm, I know the mechanics of everything. I've seen the mating of just about every animal except a man and woman."

"Honey, what we will do is so much more than just mating. We'll make love and no animal can do that. Trust me what we'll feel is much more than mating. Will you trust me?"

She sat on the bed and removed her boots. "As much as I can."

He sat beside her and did the same.

She stood and started to unbutton her shirt.

Travis moved in front of her and covered her hands with his. "Let me." He made quick work of her shirt unbuttoning it and sliding it down her arms. Then unlaced her chemise but he left her covered. Then he unbuttoned her pants and slid them down her legs with her bloomers, leaving her in just her chemise.

Then he undressed and stood before her.

She pulled the chemise over her head and threw it on the floor, wanting to be as naked as he was. Wanting to explore him as she knew he would explore her.

Charlie, though trying to be brave, forced herself to

keep her hands at her sides. "Travis, I don't understand these feelings I have. I want to—"

He placed two fingers over her lips. "Shh. I know what you want and what you need. You said you'd trust me."

"Yes, I wouldn't have agreed if I didn't."

He took her lips gently with his for just a moment and then broke away. "Thank you, for believing in me."

Her heart pounded and her pulse raced. Her desire to touch him warred with her need to be touched by him. She lifted her hand to his face and cupped his jaw. "You're my husband. I have to learn to have faith in you and this is a good way to start."

He bent and swept her into his arms, took her to the bed and laid her in the middle. Then he came down next to her, resting his weight on a bent arm and using his free hand to caress her arm, rubbing up and down. Then he moved to her stomach and on down her body, leaving tingling, fiery sparks wherever his fingers touched her.

She reached over and ran her hands through the sparse and curly hairs on his chest, each one seeming to want to circle around her fingers and stop her progress. He had a large scar on his chest and she explored it gently with her fingers.

"How did you get this? Were you shot?"

"Yes, but it doesn't matter now. I'll tell you later."

Charlie nodded and ran a hand over his shoulder and

down his arm, enjoying the feel of his muscles as he stroked her body.

"Travis, I need—"

He kissed her stomach again, moved lower and finally, he relieved her wanting as she shattered her completion.

Then he covered her with his body and the whole magnificent dance started again.

———

Smiling, feeling lazy and totally relaxed, Charlie cuddled into Travis' side. They lay in the bed, covered with the two blankets, though she had her leg out on top, crossing over his.

"Tell me about your scar. Why were you shot?"

He wrapped his arm around her shoulders as she lay next to him. "You know what I used to do, but it sounds like you only got part of the story. That last company we acquired was a small business outside of Pittsburgh. The employees took umbrage at being left without a job, rightly so I might add. Anyway one of them decided to take matters in his own hands. He decided if he eliminated me, he would eliminate the acquisition. He didn't realize that another lawyer would just come in and finish what I started."

"So he shot you?"

"Yes. He lay in wait for me to return to my hotel

room and shot me in the hallway. Luckily for me, he was a poor shot. Even at close range he didn't kill me."

She kissed his chest. "At this moment, I'm glad he was a poor shot."

He hugged her closer. "So am I. Anyway, I decided then and there I was on the wrong side if people were trying to kill me. And I thought people needed someone to help them, but I couldn't do it there, I was too well known for being the," he rolled his eyes to the side. "Other guy. Then I remembered Ian and Molly had moved to Oregon City. What better place to start up a new practice than in a new city."

She laid her head on his chest. "I guess we can't go back now, can we? We are truly married in the eyes of the law as well as God's eyes."

He lazily rubbed her back. "Do you mind so much?"

Charlie shrugged. "I don't know. I'd never figured to marry because I never planned on changing my ways and still don't." *This stance, this refusal to not change cost me my family for more than a year. Was it worth it then? Is it worth it now?* "So now, if you can't abide me as I am, you'll have to divorce me. Being a lawyer, you already knew that."

He got quiet for a moment. "I never planned on being married either. My father was a terrible man and a terrible father. He never had time for me and never wanted to make time either. I was just something that happened and was of no consequence to him. I'm afraid

I'll be like that and so hadn't planned on marrying, just to make sure."

"You won't be. I have a feeling you'll be a good father, simply because you know the kind of father you don't want to be."

"I hope you're right. We could have made a baby, you know."

Lying back, she touched her stomach. A smile slowly spread across her face. "I'm aware of that. Would you be upset?"

He thought for a moment. "I think I would be happy. I have you to remind me to be a good father if I'm becoming the cold person my sire was."

"Your sire?" She leaned up on one arm and ran the other hand through the sparse hair on his chest. "Are you a horse?"

"No, but my father was only that to my mother. Used her as a brood mare, nothing more. My sister and I were the only children he had and he married her off as soon as she turned sixteen."

"That's really sad. Up until my mother died she was devoted to my father and most of the time he seemed to love her. But he did lose his temper, mostly when he was drinking, and beat her or us for no apparent reason. I think he missed her when she passed and that's why he drank so much after she died...he was numbing the pain he felt. Of course, he still beat us if we had a thought of our own or said or did anything he didn't like. In the end, before he threw me out, he would beat me for no reason other than I was in the room with him."

He rubbed a hand over her back and caught her left hand with the other, entwining their fingers. He stared at her hand in his.

"What?"

"I must get you a ring. You need a wedding ring."

"If you get me some big gaudy thing I'll never wear it."

He cleared his throat.

She was sure that was what he'd had in mind.

"Very well, what kind would you like?"

"If I must wear one, I want a thin, plain gold band. The cheapest you can buy."

"But, no woman wants just a plain gold band. You know, I'm fairly wealthy. You can get whatever you want."

She pulled her hand from his and lay back with her arms crossed over her chest with the blanket beneath. "I told you what I want. If you get me anything else, I won't wear it."

"All right. A plain gold band it is."

He leaned up on one arm and lowered his head.

She rolled away, the talk of rings and babies making what they'd done all too real. *What am I thinking? I wanted to get to really know him, but then again, even with courting how much did one person really know another? I could just ask Ben. He'd known Emily since they were children and yet it seemed he didn't really know her at all since she'd jilted him. I need to think.* "We should get back." She dropped the blankets and picked up her clothes, pulled the chemise over her head and her bloomers up, shoved her arms in the sleeves and quickly put on her pants and socks before shoving her feet into her boots.

"You're really not like any woman I've ever known. Most women would be asking me to turn my back so they could dress in a modicum of privacy."

She quickly cinched her belt and slammed her pistols into their holsters, then tied each holster to her thighs. "I'm not like most women. You better get that through your head or we'll have problems. I can guarantee that." *If I was any more irritated, at myself for falling for his charms, I don't know what I'd do.*

Travis leaned back with his arms behind his head and watched her. "Are you good with those guns." He nodded his head toward her gun belt.

"I am. You can ask my brothers or you can challenge me to a gun fight. Your choice."

He shoved his head back onto the pillow and laughed. "I'll take your word for it. I don't need to ask your brothers."

"I'm glad you find my competency with my weapons so funny." She turned on her heel and went out the door. Once outside she lengthened her strides.

"Wait, Charlie, wait. I'm sorry."

She was about twelve feet from the door when she heard him behind her. She stopped and turned around. Travis was standing about six feet from her naked as the day he was born. Charlie started laughing. She couldn't help it.

He put his hands on his hips. "What is so funny?"

She choked back the laughter. "You. You're so concerned with me, with my feelings, you ran out without a stitch on, not knowing who could be out here. That's funny." She walked over and wrapped her arms around his neck. "And very sweet." She kissed him. Then she pulled back and dropped her arms to her sides. "Now get your clothes on so we can go home."

He turned to go back in.

She swatted his behind.

He grabbed his back side and looked over his shoulder. "Hey!"

Charlie shrugged. "I couldn't resist. Your bottom is just so perfect and needed a swat. What can I say?" She grinned.

"I married an ornery woman," he muttered as he rubbed his backside on the way to the shack.

As soon as he was inside, the smile slipped from Charlie's face. What had she gotten herself into? Travis would be all too easy to fall in love with, but she couldn't do that. She'd seen what love could do to you. Love made her father drink himself to death rather than live without her mother. She didn't ever want to feel that way...to feel that much grief.

CHAPTER SIX

Charlie and Travis arrived home and began caring for their animals.

Lois met them in the barn and stood with her arms crossed over her chest. "Where have you been?"

Charlie looked the woman up and down. She was trembling with rage and Charlie couldn't have been happier. She didn't like Lois, never had and never would. "We've been riding, not that it's any business of yours."

Lois lifted her chin. "Everything Travis does is my business. We're associates."

Charlie was very glad her hands were busy brushing Gulliver or she might have been tempted to slap the woman silly. "You're business associates. His personal life is just that...personal."

Putting her hands on her hips, Lois looked at Travis. "Where have you been? I thought we were supposed to look for an office today."

Travis narrowed his eyes and pointed at Lois. "Actually, *you* were supposed to look for an office...by yourself. I never agreed to look for one with you. And I found a house that I was moving into, but now I think you should move into it." He sighed. "Lois. Charlie and I are married. I'd feel better if you had your own place to live. Away from us."

She tilted her head and lifted her eyebrows. "Why? They have room here. I think as long as you're living here, so should I. We're associates, after all. And I'd already heard about your marriage, if you can call it that."

Travis walked to the woman and put his hands on her shoulders. His voice was gentle. "Lois, this is my family now. You are not. You must find a home of your own. You have the financial where-with-all to buy whatever house you want if you don't want the one I chose, so go find one."

Charlie finished with Gulliver and returned the curry brush to its place on the shelf between the stalls. She walked out of the stall, closing and locking the gate behind her and then turned to Lois. "If that isn't clear enough, how's this? Get out of my house. You're not welcome here. You have two weeks to find a home, then you're going to the hotel." She took Travis' hand. "Let's go to the house. I'm hungry. Your *assistant* can follow or not...her choice." Then she stopped and turned around. "If I ever see or hear you refer to Travis as anything but your business assistant again, you'll have to deal with me and that won't be fun for you."

"Well, I never!"

"And you never will as long as I live," said Charlie over her shoulder.

"He might have married you, but he always comes back to my bed." Lois sneered.

—————

Travis stopped walking, turned and stalked back to Lois. "Stop spreading lies, Lois."

She shoved a loose strand of hair behind her ears and turned her gaze away from him. "Why? She doesn't believe me anyway."

"There are those that would and I won't have it. Do you understand? Once more and we're through."

Her eyes widened and her jaw dropped. "You can't mean that. One little lie, that's all."

"You heard me." He turned and walked back to Charlie.

Charlie looked over at Travis as they walked. "What does she mean by that? If it's a lie, why say it in your hearing?"

He took a deep breath. "She's trying to separate us. Get you to question me as to whether I ever slept with her."

"Why would she say something like that if you've never slept with her?"

"Because she lies? I don't know. Why would you believe her? I'm your husband."

"Because I don't know you any better than I know her. For all I know she's telling the truth."

"She's not, trust me."

"I did trust you but now I wonder if I was wrong to do so. As a matter-of-fact, I think for now you should stay in your room and I'll stay in mine."

"Charlie, please. You're my wife. I won't lie to you."

"I don't know that. All I know is one of you is telling the truth, one is lying and I don't know which one is what. I think it best you don't move in with me just now" She sprinted toward the house. *I hadn't realized I'd be this sore and that horseback ride didn't help matters any.*

––––––––

Lois watched Travis walk away with Charlie. *That woman needs to be eliminated. When she's dead Travis will turn to me for comfort and then he'll be mine. But how do I kill her and make it look like an accident?*

Then she saw Charlie leave Travis behind while she jogged toward the house. *Does trouble reign in the MacGregor household? How can I take advantage of their squabble?*

––––––––

Charlie stopped outside the kitchen door and slowed her breathing. She didn't want to be breathless when she entered the kitchen, although now that she understood making love, she figured Rebecca would just assume she and Travis had been doing that. Charlie would not disabuse her of that idea.

As it was, Rebecca was not in the kitchen so Charlie had worried for nothing. As she walked to the stairs, she heard the kids outside in the front yard. It was after lunchtime and as she passed the dining room she saw Ian and Rebecca in the swing on the porch purportedly watching the children.

She continued on to her bedroom. Removing her gun belt, she hung it on a wall peg, then took off her boots and lay on the bed.

What am I to do about Travis? Do I believe him because he's my husband? Do I believe the woman who wants him, either back or for the first time? Maybe she wants to break us up figuring he'll be more open to her advances. Well, I won't make it easy for her.

She jumped up and slid on her boots to head to the kitchen to catch Travis. She didn't have to go so far, meeting him in the hallway.

"Travis. I've done some thinking and you're right, I need to believe you. You're my husband and if you don't tell me the truth, we might as well not be married. I think that's what Lois is hoping for. Well I'm not giving up on us or on our marriage, that lightly." She spoke quietly. "We may have made a baby and I don't want to raise the child on my own."

He walked over to her and wrapped his arms around her. "I'm glad you decided to believe me. I agree if we can't trust each other to tell the truth, we don't have much of a marriage. If we made a baby, I want to be here to help raise him or her."

"Do you care which it is?" She leaned back her hands on his upper arms.

He smiled and held her. "I don't care which. We'll raise them the same way. What if our daughter wants to learn to do knitting, crochet and those kinds of arts? Do you know how to do those?"

"Actually, I do. I didn't put on my guns until my father threw me out of the house, but I told you that. I was seventeen. I've had almost seven years to get proficient with them."

"Come make love with me, Charlie."

"Can't. Maybe tomorrow but I'm sore now."

He ran a finger down her cheek. "That's right. I should remember that was your first time. But you'll be better by tomorrow."

She let go of him and stepped out of his embrace. "I want you to move into my room, but not until Lois can see you do it." She looked over the railing to see if Lois was around and perhaps eavesdropping, but she didn't see anyone.

"You want to dig into her the fact we're married?"

"I want her to see that you're my husband, not her lover."

He cupped her jaw. "I was never her lover, nor do I have any desire to be."

Charlie looked into his eyes and saw the truth. She covered his hand with hers. "Good." She wrapped a hand around his neck and brought her lips to his.

The kiss was sweet until she ran her tongue lightly along the seam of his lips.

He opened.

She entered.

Travis pulled her tight to him, his need for her evident.

She stepped back. "We should probably stop since we can't make love right now."

"Oh, there are many ways to make love, which I intend to show you, but not now. Tonight."

"Yes, tonight," she breathed the words, unable to catch her breath. She heard someone coming up the stairs. "Pretend you're moving your belongings now. I believe Lois is coming."

He shook his head and tugged her close again. "This is a better way." He lowered his head again and took her lips with his.

Lois gasped and then huffed. "Can't you two do that in private?"

Charlie turned to her. "This is my house. I'll do whatever I want, anytime I want and wherever I want."

She narrowed her eyes. "Shouldn't you be looking for a house and an office?"

"I just came to get my...my shawl."

Charlie took in a short breath and exhaled it quickly. "You're already wearing your coat and it's not that cold outside that you would need a shawl, too. So, what are you really doing here?"

She lifted her chin. "Nothing...I...Travis."

Charlie lifted an eyebrow and held up a hand. "Say no more. You thought Travis would need some consoling after our spat this morning, didn't you? And you thought you'd be the perfect one to console him. Except the perfect person is me...not you."

She looked at Travis.

He had a grin from ear to ear.

Obviously hearing just what he wanted to hear from Charlie. "I'll talk to you later," she whispered for his ears only.

Lois huffed off down the hall to her room.

She stepped forward and took his hand. "Move your things to my room. You said you have lots of things to teach me, so start teaching. I have a couple of days free from hunting and chores because we got married. The family expects us to go somewhere. Do you want to go to Portland for a few days? I could show you around."

He kissed the top of her hand. "I can't. I need to get Lois settled out of this house and I need to find an office now more than ever."

She put her hands on her hips. "What do you mean? I'm not afraid of her."

Chuckling, he shook his head slowly. "I know, but I don't need my wife shooting my business assistant."

"Well, there is that." Then she frowned. "I'm telling you something is wrong with that woman."

"She's not harmful, just tedious to be around. She is a very good assistant though."

"Well, if you're to find her a home and an office, you'd better get going. I'll go do my chores in the barn. It's my week to muck the stalls."

He raised his eyebrows. "How could you put that off?"

"I'd switch with Peter or Ben but now I don't have to so it's a moot point."

"I'm sorry. We'll take a few days after she's out of here."

"She'll still have you under her thumb, she's your assistant and she can do lots of things to mess up your business. And you can't have that, so you'll stay around to keep track of her. It's okay. Business is business." She turned and headed out to the barn with a stop in the kitchen for a couple of sugar cubes.

She began her duties by mucking Gulliver's stall. Next to Ian's Pegasus, Gulliver was the largest horse they owned. She'd picked him out when he was a foal. Ben and Rebecca already had their horses and so this foal was hers. His dame was an Appaloosa and so was he. He was a beautiful horse from the time he was a colt she knew he would be amazing. He was golden with white hind end and a white blaze. His belly and legs were blond except for the four white socks.

"Hi there, Gulliver, old boy. I've got something special." She reached into her leather coat pocket and pulled out a single sugar cube. She laid it in the palm of her hand and put her hand open so her palm was taut and smooth. She didn't want him to bite her by mistake. "What do you think of that? You like sugar cubes don't you? Hmm?" She rubbed his head up and down from the forehead to the nose.

"Males always like sugar," a voice said from behind her.

Charlie took a deep breath and sighed before turning around. "What do you want, Lois?"

"I came to warn you. You should get this marriage annulled while you still can."

Charlie smiled. "What makes you think it could be annulled?"

"Travis always moves slow to begin with. You haven't been together long enough."

"Just because he hasn't slept with you yet doesn't mean he moves slow. As a matter of fact, we would have to get a divorce now, not an annulment." She turned away to open the gate to Pegasus' stall.

"No!" Lois ran at her, surprising Charlie. Her fingernails dug into Charlie's face.

Charlie threw her off and, her face burning where Lois' nails had dug in, drew her gun.

Lois froze on the ground where she lay.

"You will go to the house, pack your bags and move to the hotel immediately. I won't tell anyone you did this, if you move." Holding still and not shaking with the rage flowing through her took most of Charlie's concentration. Most but not all. She could still shoot if she needed to. "If you don't, or you make any hints that the move is anything but your idea, I will tell them what happened and have you arrested for assault. Do you understand? If you ever try to harm me or any of my family, I'll kill you. Do you understand?"

Lois stayed on the ground and nodded, wide-eyed.

"Say it. I want to hear that you understand and will be out of the house within an hour."

Lois stood and crossed her arms over her chest. "I understand and will be gone from the house in an hour...or less."

"And you will not talk to Travis or anyone else other than to say it's time for you to find a place of your own and being at the hotel is better. That's all. Understand? I don't want this to come back on Travis. I won't have you hurting his business by your violence."

She dropped her arms to her sides but her hands formed fists. "Yes, I understand."

Charlie knew, if given the opportunity, Lois would attack again. She didn't lower her gun. "Now get out. I don't want to see your face in my home again."

Lois turned and stomped out.

She holstered her gun. Only then did Charlie place

the back of her hand against her face. It came away covered in blood. She needed to get her face cleaned and get the dirt from Lois' nails out of the wound.

Now she had to figure out what to tell the family. They wouldn't let this go.

CHAPTER SEVEN

Charlie went inside and got a washcloth from the drawer next to the sink. She pumped cold water onto the cloth and pressed it to her face. The cold felt wonderful against her heated skin.

"Charlie? What's the matter? What happened?" Travis walked to her side.

"Nothing. I tripped and fell in the barn, that's all."

"Here let me see."

As much as she didn't want him to see, she couldn't avoid it. Eventually he would see her face and the long grooves in her face made by Lois' fingernails.

He touched her cheek and his eyes shot wide. "What the hell happened?"

"Nothing. I told you. I fell." *I hate not telling him the truth, but I don't want him to do anything that would harm his business and firing Lois just after he and I married, would cause the gossips tongues to wag.*

His mouth formed a thin line and his eyes narrowed. "You didn't fall. I doubt you've ever fallen in a barn in your life. Those are fingernail marks. Lois did this to you. I'll make her pay for this. I'll—"

Charlie laid two fingers over his lips. "I'm pleased you want to avenge me, but I've handled it. She's moving to the hotel as we speak and she won't be back."

He kissed her fingers. "I'm firing her as an assistant."

She cupped his jaw. "This is the end of it. She'll be gone from our personal lives and that's what matters."

He leaned into her hand. "I'm so sorry this happened to you. She's a bit unhinged when it comes to me."

"What makes you think it was you that set her off?"

He tilted his head and lifted a brow. Then he closed his arms around her waist. "Are you telling me it wasn't?"

Charlie chuckled and shook her head, her cheek still hurt but she was getting used to the feeling. "She was incensed that we'd need a divorce not an annulment."

"Ah, the truth will out. I told you, I've never slept with her."

"So you did."

He dropped his hands to his sides and reached for her cheek. "She still should not have attacked you. I can't have that. I have to do something."

She moved away, cloth at cheek. "Please, Travis, let it go. I don't want to have to kill her and if she attacks me again, I might have to. But that's less likely if she still works with you."

"I suppose that solution makes some sense. I'll leave it for now, but I don't have to be friendly, just civil."

"Yes, just civil. Now I have to scrub this and get it clean. It's not pretty and I'm not pretty while doing it. It hurts, so why don't you go elsewhere for a while?"

"No."

She shook her head and narrowed her eyes. "What?"

"I'm not leaving you to go through this by yourself. I can help."

"You can't and you'll only distract me. If I let you clean this you won't know how much pain I can take and what I can't. You'll be too easy and I need to get it clean, so just go about your chores and leave me alone."

"All right. I don't like it but you make sense." He kissed her on the forehead and left the room.

Charlie got the basin and dipped some water into it from the bucket they kept on the stove with the coffee. It was always at least warm. Now, it was hot, and she added cold water until it was just bearable. She took the lye soap and scrubbed her cheek. It hurt like hell. "Owww, gosh darn it." She rinsed the area and put witch hazel on the injury with a small, double-thick piece of cotton cloth and sucked in breaths to control the pain. Then she covered the area with a thin coat of honey.

After cleaning the basin, she went in search of Travis and found him reading in the living room.

"All done. It'll scar, you know."

His mouth turned down and he put the book on the coffee table before going to her. "So? It won't detract from your beauty if that's what you're worried about."

"I don't want to seem vain, but yes, I'd worried you would be put off by them."

"Nothing could put me off of you."

"Do you think we'll ever love each other?"

Shaking his head, he slowly released her. "I can't. It has nothing to do with you. It's all me. It's my problem."

She held her hands behind her back so he wouldn't see how nervous this conversation made her and yet she needed to know. "Tell me about it."

Travis shrugged and walked to the window. "I was engaged to my childhood sweetheart. We'd been planning to marry for as long as I can remember. I'd loved her for years. Then she was gone."

"She married someone else?"

He stood his side to the window. He ran his hands down his face. "I wish. No, she was raped and murdered by an escaped convict."

Charlie's hand flew to her mouth. "Oh, my God. I'm so sorry. Was the man caught?"

"Yes," he clenched his jaw and looked out the window. "And then he was hanged for his crimes. I watched every twitch he made until they cut him down. I wanted to make sure he was dead."

Charlie walked up to him, his back to her, and put

her arms around him. "I can't imagine what you must have felt. Maybe even what you still feel, but I hope you won't push me away because of it." *I have to protect my heart. If he can't love me, maybe we should divorce now.*

She released him and slipped out of the living room, heading back to the barn. The smell of the hay and the horses soothed her and allowed her to think. She climbed into the loft where she had a blanket so she could lie down.

Now as she lay in the loft, chewing on a piece of hay, she wondered how she could help Travis. He needed her help; she knew it. She knew that somewhere in him was the ability to love her, but she didn't know how to make him realize that fact. Realize no one probably would murder her. That she was capable of taking care of herself, though Lois attacked her, she repelled the attack with her gun.

Travis called from the floor of the barn. "Charlie? Are you here?"

She stood and walked to the edge of the loft. "Up here."

He climbed into the loft. "I figured I'd find you in the barn, but didn't expect to have to climb a ladder to get to you."

Charlie walked back to the blanket and sat.

Travis followed her. "May I?"

"Suit yourself." She laid back bracing her body with her arms, elbows bent. She waited until he was settled next to her. "Why'd you come out here?"

"Because you did. I can't leave things between us the way we did. We're in this marriage whether we want to be or not. Divorce isn't an option for me. Not now, not ever. I watched my parent's divorce and though I got more attention from Mother I also know she was miserable. Though Father wouldn't admit it, so was he. I won't go through that."

He leaned over and with a thumb and forefinger turned her head to face him. "Understand Charlie? You're stuck with me."

She pulled her chin from his hand. "Don't tell me what I can and can't do. If I want to divorce you I will. I bet Lois would file the paperwork for me for free."

Travis smiled. Then he chuckled. Then he laughed out right and fell to his back.

Charlie stared and then she chuckled and shook her head before she began laughing, too. "We're quite the pair. We haven't even given our marriage a chance and we're discussing whether we can get divorced or not. That's crazy. We're crazy."

"Agreed."

"So what do we do now?"

"What we were doing. I'm moving into your room, and we're beginning our married life."

"We'll look for a place of our own after you find an office and maybe Lois will move into that one you found, but I wouldn't count on it. She won't do it, just to spite me, but she can't stay at the hotel forever, although I'd be perfectly fine with her going broke from living at the hotel."

"Don't say that. As my associate, she's entitled to half the business and I can't buy her out...yet. She invested in me when I couldn't afford to expand my office."

"Okay, so finding the witch a house is first, then the office second, then our house third."

"What shall we do with the rest of the day?"

"Well, I suggest we get started finding a house for your assistant and let's not make it too nice."

Travis laughed.

She was right. Lois eschewed the house Travis had picked out. And Charlie knew why. It was ugly. Dark colors inside and out, not enough windows. It was horrible.

Yet after looking at several houses for sale, Charlie couldn't find one she liked for Lois. They were either too nice or too ugly. She didn't want her living in a hovel, all that would do is build resentment and that was something she really did want to avoid, didn't she?

One week later

Travis took Lois out to look at houses, without Charlie. He wanted to talk to Lois.

As they walked along side-by-side, he glanced at her and she had a smile on her face.

He continued to walk slowly. "Lois, we need to talk. I know you attacked Charlie. I won't put up with it. Charlie has asked me not to fire you but I will and damned the agreement we have about the business. I'll see you in jail and the business ownership will be moot at that point."

Her eyebrows became slashes and her eyes narrowed so much they almost closed. "She said she wouldn't tell you. You're just upset because her beauty is marred—"

"Charlie didn't tell me. You just did. I was only guessing before. What I said stands. Now, I believe you can find your own home. You have the money and you'll be responsible for the maintenance of the house you live in. I'm headed home to my wife, who will always be beautiful to me."

Two days later

The first house Charlie and Travis looked at that day was, they thought, perfect for Lois. Two bedrooms, living room and kitchen. Small but cozy. This was the fifth house they'd looked at. Finding the perfect place was harder than she thought possible. The population of the town wasn't large, but the turnover of homes happened with regularity. But this home looked like a good one.

The house was yellow with dark brown shutters on the windows. The rest of the trim and the small porch out front were all painted the same color as the shutters. As a matter of fact, the paint job appeared fresh.

"We need to at least have her look at it before we talk to the owner," said Travis.

"Well, if she doesn't like it you can turn it into your law offices. It will be perfect. You each have an office, plus access to a waiting room and a kitchen."

He tapped his chin. "Hmm. I hadn't thought about that, but you're right it would be perfect. Let's tell Max we'll take it and then look at the next one. The bigger of the bedrooms is mine."

"Of course. I can't let her be too happy. I still want her to go back where she came from. I've already made my position very clear to her, but maybe you'd better check and make sure she understands."

"I'll talk to her about that and numerous other things. I already talked to her about her attack on you. She thinks I'm upset because she marred your beauty, which I am, but I'm angry she could even let her jealousy come to that. I will never love her. No need for you to be jealous."

"I'm not jealous. She is. And you'll never convince her of that you won't love her and saying 'I'll never love her will only make her try harder."

"I don't intend to discuss anything to her that is not work related and she's lucky I'm not closing the business altogether."

She cupped his jaw. "You're a good person, Travis MacGregor, much better than I am."

"You are, too, or you would have killed her for injuring you."

Cold permeated the February air as they walked south along Main Street and then turned west on Maple Street and went two streets over to Oak Street. They could see their breath as they walked.

On the corner of Oak and Maple was a large, beautiful, two-story house painted blue with white shutters. The porch had a rail about half-way, up the eight-foot support columns, which were actually the trunks of small trees with the bark scraped off and painted white. Below the rail was a cross-hatch of wood. All the rails and the cross-hatch were painted white, but the floor of the porch was natural wood.

Charlie stopped in front of the home. "This is a very nice house from the outside. Can we go inside?"

Travis spread his arm in a wide arc toward the building. "I have the key. Max gave it to me for this one and the last one we looked at. After you, my dear."

She giggled and curtsied. "Thank you, kind sir."

After he opened the gate in the four-foot tall white picket fence, he took her hand and tucked it in the crook of his elbow.

They entered into the foyer between the living room and the dining room. Back of the dining room was the kitchen. A four-burner stove with green porcelain doors and brass handles stood on one wall. The wall opposite them was lined with cupboards, held the sink with a pump and the icebox. To their left was a mud room and door to the back yard. Charlie loved this set-up. Though she didn't like to cook if she had to, doing it in a nice, bright kitchen made it more pleasurable.

A door in the right side of the kitchen from the front door led to a small bedroom.

Behind the living room was a small library or perhaps Travis could have his office in the room.

The stairs went up off the foyer. At the top was a long hall with two doors on either side. Two of the bedrooms were fairly small. They would hold a double bed and a bureau or chest of drawers but not both. Pegs on the wall served for hanging clothes, as both rooms were without closets.

The master bedroom was huge by comparison and Charlie fell in love. She'd always had a small room. Even at the current house, next to the guest room, hers was the smallest bedroom.

This room was two of her bedroom at home. A double bed, bureau, nightstands and chest of drawers would all fit easily in the room. It also had a reasonably sized closet.

Next to the master bedroom was a very small room that could serve as a sewing room, had Charlie been inclined to sew. Or it could be a nursery, if they should have children.

"Travis. I adore this house. I want it for us."

"All right. We'll buy it. Whatever will make you happy is what we'll do."

"You say that now because we're newly married and you want to make love to me. What if having you love me is what makes me happy? Will you try to love me then?"

"I—"

She shook her head and put her hands up in front of her. "Never mind. I shouldn't have brought it up. We haven't known each other long enough to be in love with the other."

His mouth turned down and the look in his eyes was sad. "No, we haven't, but I don't believe it's an emotion I can feel. Never again."

She laid her hand on his arm. "Don't push me away because of what happened to your fiancée. That will never happen to me."

He patted her hand. "But then we just never know, do we?"

Charlie snatched back her hand. "What kind of thing is that to say? Do you wish that fate upon me so you can be proved right? Is being right all you care about?"

"No, of course, not. That's not what I meant at all. I meant...ah heck," he ran his hand behind his neck. "I don't know what I meant."

She sighed and furrowed her brows. "I'm not asking that you love me. I'm asking you to be open to the idea."

"I can't. I'm sorry." He walked downstairs and then out the front door.

She knew he was about to buy the house because she wanted it. Why couldn't she have just left it at that? Why bring up love? Because she was falling hard and fast for her husband and he wasn't even considering the possibility he could be falling in love with her.

CHAPTER EIGHT

Because the house was empty and the owners had signed all the necessary paperwork signing the house over to the Oregon City Bank, Charlie and Travis moved into their new home a week later. They'd brought the furniture from Charlie's bedroom but had bought everything else at the furniture store in Portland as no furniture store existed in Oregon City.

A couple of things they'd had made, including a bassinette for their first child should they have one.

I haven't had my menses since we got married and we've been married for right at six weeks. Am I pregnant? Charlie's hands rubbed her still flat stomach. *Was it possible I got pregnant from our first time making love? I need to go see Doc Wade. He can tell me for sure.*

Concern written all over his face, Travis asked, "Are you happy about the possibility of a child?"

She dropped her hand back to her side and turned

her head rather than at him. "I don't know yet how I feel. I never thought I'd be having children. Of course, I never thought I'd be married either."

He stepped forward and took her hands in his. "We'll make great parents. You'll see. You'll teach them to fight and shoot. I'll teach them about the law so they'll be prepared if they should ever get arrested for fighting or shooting someone."

Charlie chuckled and then laughed outright. "You have an answer for everything, which is good in your line of work."

Travis laughed, too. "I'm supposed to have the answers. That's why people hire me."

"Yes, I suppose that's true."

"Will you give up your guns and take up domestic chores now that you're expecting?"

She dropped his hands. "No. Don't try to change me, Travis. It won't work. I'll do as I please."

"You have a child to think about now. I think it's time you dressed and acted like a woman."

"You don't mind how I dress or act when you're making love to me." She stopped for a moment and put a finger to her chin while narrowing her eyes. "Oh, wait, I just remembered, you can't love me, and so we're just having relations aren't we?. You said you wouldn't try to change me. That you accepted me as I am. Was that a lie?"

He tilted his head and furrowed his brows. "Now, Charlie, I'm not really trying to change you. I simply want you to see other possibilities. And we're still friends, so I'd say it's making love."

"I wouldn't. And I think you should probably sleep on the sofa until you get straight in your mind what love is."

He shook his head and put his hands on his hips. "I'm not sleeping on the sofa."

"Fine, then I will. Either way we are not having relations anytime soon." She stalked from the room and headed outside to their barn, by way of the kitchen so she could grab a carrot, for a soothing talk with Gulliver.

Since she married, she'd taken to wearing her braided hair outside her shirt rather than inside. She didn't care anymore to look more like a man. Now, she walked with such long, determined strides that the braid swung on her back, sweeping back and forth across the top of her butt.

She walked to the big Appaloosa's stall and made nickering sounds before opening the gate.

"Hi, boy. How are you today?" She reached into her pocket, pulled out the carrot and fed it to him. "You like that do you? Yes, I knew you did." She petted his soft nose and then his neck before scratching behind his ears. "What am I to do with him, huh boy? I can't leave him now, though I probably wouldn't have before this pregnancy came around. See, I'm falling in love with my husband. What kind of fool does that make me?"

Gulliver nuzzled her with his nose on her shoulder. She knew it was his way of comforting her. Charlie got the curry comb and worked on his coat, taking off the loose hair and dirt before she used the brush to make his coat shine. After she was done with that she checked his hooves, gently pulling on his fetlock until he raised his hoof and she could clean it with the pick.

When she was done grooming Gulliver, she patted his nose. "Thanks for listening, boy. Even if you can't say anything, just talking to you helps."

She left the barn and strolled back to the house, meeting Travis halfway.

"I was getting worried about you. You've been gone for over an hour."

"I groomed Gulliver. He's all pretty now."

He put his hands on his hips. "So you thought grooming him was more important than our conversation?"

"Our *conversation* was done. I'm not changing and you shouldn't try to change me."

"I probably shouldn't but I'll also probably try again to get you to be more womanly for the child's sake if not yours. You won't be able to wear your pants as you increase. You'll have to wear a dress then."

"Pants come in all sizes and suspenders work just fine. Haven't you ever seen a fat man? He must buy his pants somewhere."

"I suppose that's true, but would you at least think about it?

"When it happens that I can't wear my pants at all, I might let you take me to the dressmaker and buy me dresses, until then, leave me be."

"Fair enough."

"I should think so." She continued to the house, her strides long and fast. Charlie didn't want to fight anymore and it seemed that was all they did lately.

Once in the house, she kept going right out the front door, headed for the mercantile. She was in the mood to see the local kids and the candy always brought them out. She'd been lax about doing it every week, it having been since just after she married that she did the last one.

She came out of the store and she whistled. The kids started coming like everything was the same. Everything in their lives was the same, except Charlie and she'd fallen down on the job. Well, that would stop now. She'd do this again next week and every week after.

This time, she ran into Lois coming up the walk to their house.

"What do you want, Lois?"

The black haired woman lifted her chin. "Nothing from you. I'm here to see Travis."

"Fine. He should have returned from the barn by now." Charlie walked past her without another word. She had a strange throbbing in the scar on her face as though it knew Lois was near. Before she could stop herself, she lifted her hand to her face and touched the scar. It seemed fine, no spontaneous bleeding or other damage from Lois' presence.

Charlie lengthened her strides to get away from the evil woman without seeming to run at least until she was out of sight. She reached the mercantile in about five minutes rather than ten.

When she entered the store, the bell above the door rang. "Hi, George," she called to the eldest son of the owner, who stood behind the counter.

"Hi, Charlie." He moved the candy jars to the top of the counter. "Here for candy, I bet."

Charlie smiled as she sidled up to the counter and leaned on it. "Yup I need thirty candy sticks."

"Pick out the ones you want, I'll keep those for your family, separate." He winked.

Charlie laughed. "Your father has been telling you my secrets."

George chuckled and nodded. "He wanted me to be prepared when you came in."

"Well, good." She counted the jars. "Sixteen today. Looks like you have a couple of new flavors."

George smiled and put his hands on two of the jars. "We just got butterscotch and cherry."

"Yum, I love butterscotch. Give me two of each except, skip the peppermint and give me four of the butterscotch. Put two of those in my bag and the rest in the bag for the kids. Put one of each of the other flavors in my bag, too."

"You got it." He made quick work of gathering the candy. "That'll be a buck fifty, please."

Charlie handed him the money and picked up the two bags. The one for her she put in the inside pocket of her coat. When she reached the boardwalk outside the store a dozen kids waited and more were coming. She whistled to let the other kids know she was there with candy.

"Here we go, children. You know the rules only one candy stick. If you take more than one, you won't get any more again."

"Miss Charlie," said Clifford, a red headed boy of about ten. "My little brother Calvin, is sick and couldn't come. Can I take one for him?"

"I wondered where he was. Yes, you may pick a candy stick for him. I know he likes the orange ones."

"Oh, yes, ma'am, that's his favorite."

Charlie reached in the bag and pulled out the last orange stick before any other child could grab it. "Here you go. Tell Calvin I hope he feels better soon."

"I will ma'am."

"Remember I'm just Charlie, not a ma'am. Okay?"

Clifford smiled wide. "Yes, ma...I mean, Charlie."

She ruffled his hair. "Go on home and give Calvin his candy. Maybe it will make him feel better."

The boy nodded and scampered off.

"I'm going to start keeping a candy jar on my desk at work. That way when you want to give away candy, you can just get it from the jar or tell the kids and have them come get it from me."

Travis came up next to her and stood with his coat behind his hands which were in his pockets.

"Why would I want to do that? I enjoy giving the kids their candy and they enjoy getting it from me."

Travis held up his hands in front of him. "Just an idea."

"Maybe if I get too big when I'm expecting to hand out the candy then I'll tell them to go see you. Or actually you'll have to tell them. It may be a good idea for you to come with me the next few months and give out the candy, too. That way they can get used to seeing you."

"All right. That bodes well, considering our earlier conversation. I figured you'd be talking to Lois about a divorce."

Feeling a pinch in her chest, she turned to him. "I don't want a divorce. We'll disagree, have fights about different things, but that doesn't mean I'll divorce you. You might have to sleep on the couch, but that's all. Everyone has disagreements. Even Rebecca and Ian do. I thought they had the perfect marriage until I got up early one morning and found Ian on the sofa. I guess she was very angry, but I never found out what about."

She gave the last child the last stick of candy and then turned to face him.

"I'm glad." He took her hands in his. "I want us to

stay married, not just because of a child but because it's the right thing to do."

"There you go again with that word. The *right* thing to do."

"What is so wrong about wanting to be right? It's my job. I have to be on the correct side of the law in order to defend my clients. They come to me because I'm defending their rights. Even Lois with her questionable morality has to do the same by her clients as I do. Prove they are not in the wrong."

"I know what your job is." She took his arm and leaned into him while they walked. "I just don't want your work to interfere with us at home. Leave it at the office. Give me some leeway and know that I might be *right*, too."

He patted her hand where it lay on his arm. "Okay, I'll do my best to leave the office at the office. How's that?"

"Great." *Now if Lois would just leave Oregon City, I'd be happy.*

———

Charlie left the house at nine o'clock the next morning and walked to the doctor's office. She wanted confirmation of her pregnancy.

She entered his office and sat in the waiting room with two other patients. The room was pleasant enough. The walls were painted white and the furniture was typical for a living room. A sofa and four Queen Anne chairs formed a circle around a short coffee table.

The table had three books on it. Charlie picked up one—Herman Melville's *Moby Dick*. She flipped to the first page in the book and started reading. The time passed quickly as she read. The story was fascinating. It was about a ship captain's obsession with a giant, white whale. Forty-five minutes later, Doc called her back. She hated to put down the book and took it with her.

"Doc, I'd like to borrow your book. I'll bring it back, I promise."

"Sure go on and take it. Now, tell me what brings you in here today."

Charlie looked down at her lap. "This is embarrassing, but I might be expecting. I haven't had one mense since we got married."

Doc nodded. "That is generally the reason for skipping your menses. Let me take a look." He went over to the counter with drawers below and cupboards above. From one of the cupboards, he took a sheet and handed it to her.

"Undress from the waist down and cover yourself with this sheet. I'll be back in a few minutes."

She hated this part of the examination though she knew it was the only way he could tell her for certain was to examine her.

Doc came back and examined her. "Are your breasts tender?"

"Yes, they are."

"I'd say you are definitely pregnant. When was your last menses?"

"About two months ago, I guess. I've been married for a little over six weeks and haven't had one in that time."

"Then I would say you are probably four to six weeks pregnant. You can expect your baby around the first of November."

She sat up with the sheet still covering her legs and placed a hand on her stomach. "A baby."

Doc smiled. "Yes, a baby. I hope you and Travis are very happy."

"Oh, we are, Doc, we are."

"Good. Now I'll let you get dressed and then we can discuss what you need to do to keep you, and the baby, healthy."

"Sure. Sure."

After he left, Charlie sat for a few moments, then she smiled, and rubbed her stomach. "Well, little MacGregor, your daddy and I are already anxious for you to be here and we love you very much. Now if I could just convince your daddy to love your mama, too."

Slipping off the table, she dressed and went in search of the doctor, finding him in his office.

"Well, Doc." She sat in one of the wooden chairs with a pretty scroll back. "What do you want me to know?"

"It's pretty simple really. I want you to drink two glasses of milk every day and just eat a good rounded diet the rest of the time. If you eat liver a few times a week, that would be good, too."

Shaking her head, she lifted her hand. "Stop right there. No way is that nasty tasting stuff going in my mouth."

Doc chuckled. "All right no liver. Just do the best you can. Plenty of meat and eggs, vegetables and even bread. I want it well rounded."

"I'll do my best." *What he wants me to eat fits with what I normally do anyway.*

"Good. Congratulations to you and Travis."

"Thanks, Doc. What do I owe you?"

"Two dollars for today. One dollar for the rest of your visits. I want to see you once a month from now until I tell you otherwise." He took out his appointment calendar. I'll see you again on March 20th at ten-thirty in the morning."

"Okay. I'll add it to the calendar." She stood, took the coins from her pocket and paid him. Then she shook his hand and walked out of the building.

Will Travis be happy now that it's certain I'm expecting? I know someone who won't be. Lois.

CHAPTER NINE

Charlie walked toward home, running her finger through the end of her braid as she walked. *Expecting. November. I really will be a mother.*

"Well, if it isn't Miss Fancy Pants and I do mean pants. After the Valentine Day dance I know why you wear pants...you don't know how to wear a dress like a lady."

Charlie stopped, looked up and saw Lois standing in front of the butcher shop window. She glanced her up and down. "You're one to talk. Lady? You? Not hardly. Besides it didn't take a lady to capture Travis' attention. Just a real woman."

Lois screamed and ran at Charlie.

Charlie pulled her right pistol and aimed it at the screaming woman.

She halted in her tracks.

"You wouldn't shoot me."

"Don't try me." Charlie lifted her hand to her cheek and touched the still-red marks there.

The woman backed up a step. "I saw you come out of the doctor's office. Is it too much to hope you are terminally ill?"

Charlie laughed. "One thing I have to say for you, is that you have a way with a phrase. But, no, I'm not dying."

Lois frowned.

"Much to your disappointment, I see. Actually, I received some very good news and I'm sure after I share it with Travis, he'll want to share it with you first."

"Good news? From the doctor?"

Charlie watched as the woman's eyes widened and then narrowed.

Lois shook her head. "No. It can't be. There is no way. Not so soon."

Charlie laughed. "Oh, but I can most certainly be. Travis can't keep his hands off me. Unlike you who has had years to attract him and couldn't. Maybe you should just go back to work. Travis does say you're very good at that, if nothing else."

She growled but stayed where she was.

Charlie finally put her weapon away. Without another word she turned and continued her walk home.

"Travis. Travis. I'm back from seeing the doctor." She called as she walked toward the kitchen.

He came out of the living room, gathered her in his arms and greeted her with a kiss. "What did he say?"

"I'm expecting around mid-November."

"A little MacGregor." He picked her up, swung her in a circle, and then let her slide down his body. "Are you happy?"

She kept her arms around his neck. "Yes. Unexpectedly, yes." Charlie placed her lips on his. The kiss was carnal, needy and all-consuming.

Travis carried her to their bedroom, never breaking the kiss.

Finally, reluctantly, she pulled away. Breathing hard, she nonetheless grinned at Travis and began shedding her clothes. By the time she was done, so was he.

He walked her backwards and when she ran into the mattress with her knees, he pushed them backward onto the bed.

He braced himself with his arms so he wouldn't crush her. Then he kissed her and made love to her. A frenzied meshing of bodies followed by a gentle one.

After having made love twice, Charlie was exhausted. She cuddled into Travis' side and immediately fell asleep.

———

Travis looked down at his sleeping wife. How had he managed to get so lucky. She was not only beautiful, she was capable, feisty, and more loving than he thought she realized.

He was very glad they'd bought this house and

weren't still living at the mansion. Too many people. He couldn't have carried her to bed and made love twice, in the middle of the day, had they still been living in the family home.

Charlotte...Charlie...was amazing. Lois had marred Charlie's face, leaving three fairly deep scars, but she'd turned the other cheek, so to speak, and wouldn't allow Travis to dissolve the agreement. Perhaps she was right. It would only infuriate Lois and she'd try something even worse than simply scratching Charlie's face.

He ran his fingers down Charlie's back. She cuddled tighter to him, so he put his arm around her and held her tight.

Would they always be this way? He couldn't imagine being without Charlie now. Whenever he tried, he felt a great sorrow and fear overtake him so he stopped imagining the possibility of her leaving. Was this love? Real love? The kind that would take them through the years into old age and beyond? Travis thought so. He'd felt something like this with Amy before she was murdered.

Surprised to find himself capable of loving again after Amy, he realized he loved Charlie, but did she love him?

With Travis gone to work, Charlie saddled Gulliver and road back to the family home to tell Rebecca her news. She could have walked but riding took half the time since the house she and Travis bought was at the southern end of town and the family home was about a mile from the north end of town.

Gracie was only about seven months old now. She'd be about fifteen months when Charlie's baby was born. Would they be friends or adversaries? She wouldn't be able to tell until they got older, but she hoped for friends. Charlie wanted to spend as much time with Rebecca as possible. She had a thousand questions and, since Rebecca had just been through the ordeal of birth, she was the person to ask.

When she reached the house, an old mansion Ian was in the process of repairing, she slid from the saddle and tied Gulliver to the hitching rail. As she walked up the path she looked at the cold, gray sky. There would be rain soon. Suddenly chilled, she flipped up the collar of her sheepskin coat. She'd either have to make the visit short or ask Peter to take Gulliver to the barn.

Entering the house, she removed her gloves and put them in the pockets of her coat. "Rebecca?" Not getting an answer, Charlie headed to the kitchen, where it sounded like a party was happening. Children's laughter, interspersed with adult guffaws emanated from the room.

She went through the door and found three seven-year-olds giggling, Ian at the end of the table making silly faces, Rebecca opposite Ian, holding Gracie, and Peter across from the children, shaking his head.

"What did I miss?" Charlie got a cup and filled it with coffee from the pot on the stove.

"Charlie!" Rebecca rose and hurried over to hug her sister with one arm and hold Gracie with the other.

"Hi, Becca." Charlie hugged her back.

"What brings you to our doorstep, this fine day?" Ian wrapped Charlie in his arms for a hug.

"I have some news that I wanted to share."

Rebecca put Gracie to her shoulder and patted her little back. "Well, what is this news that couldn't wait until Sunday dinner? Are you hungry now? We're having leftover pork roast from last night."

Gracie chewed on her hand, then grinned at Charlie and held out her arms.

Her heart overflowed with love for Gracie. I can't wait until my child makes the same gesture to me.

Charlie took the baby from Rebecca. "No, thanks, I'm fine." Then she grinned. "I'm expecting. I just found out this morning."

Rebecca clapped her hands. "Oh, that's just wonderful. Isn't that wonderful, Ian."

"It is," agreed her brother-in-law. "What did Travis say?"

Charlie smiled and sat at the table next to Peter. "He's happy, thrilled as a matter of fact, which is something that surprised me. Say, where is Ben?"

"He's gone to see Rachel Trowbridge." Rebecca grinned and looked from side to side before saying in a loud whisper. "I think he'll ask to court her. He's been enamored with her since we were on the wagon train but too shy to approach her. She is a beautiful girl. She'd be the first redhead in the family."

Charlie clapped her hands. "Oh, I'm so happy for him. He needs to marry. I know he wants children and you two are twenty-four now. It's time he took a wife and became a father. Just as long as it's not Lois."

"She was just a passing fancy. When she didn't get the response she wanted from Travis to her attending the dance with Ben, she dropped poor Ben like a hot potato." Rebecca grinned. "I was never so happy in my life."

Charlie and Ian laughed.

"I'm never getting married," said Peter.

Charlie turned her head and looked at her younger brother. "I thought that too and look at me. Why don't you want to get married?"

He smiled and sat straighter. "I'm joining the Army. I'll be a general someday."

Ian forked a bite of his leftover pork roast. "That is a hard life your choosing."

Peter nodded. "I know. But I want to serve and I know better than to ask a woman to take up that life with me."

Charlie thought for a moment, staring at her brother. *He really wants to do this. I guess the best thing is to agree and wish him well in his endeavor. Maybe he'll change his mind over the next three years, at least before he's eighteen.* "Well if that's what you really want, I'll support your decision. Who knows you may fall for an Army nurse or someone else that has chosen that life as well."

Rebecca swung her head toward Charlie, her eyes wide. "You will?"

"You will? Really? You're not kidding me?" asked Peter, giving her an incredulous look.

Charlie nodded. "Nope, I'm not kidding you. I support you in your endeavor. I want you to have your dream and if this hard life is what you choose, so be it."

Peter's smiled, but it was just a small upturn at the corner of his mouth. Then he went back to his lunch.

Charlie knew he was thinking about not joining, now that he didn't get his sisters begging him not to go, as he expected. Perhaps he would at least think twice about it before he joined something like the Army.

Ian looked over at Charlie. "What did Lois say? Or does she know yet?"

"Oh, she knows. She saw me coming out of the doctor's office. She hoped I was there for something terminal and when I told her I had happy news, she screeched and ran at me. I had to draw my weapon. That stopped her. It was sad really."

"That's not your fault. Travis had the good luck to have to marry you." Ian wiped his mouth with his napkin and placed it on the empty plate in front of him. "I'm of the opinion we only have to marry those we love anyway or we wouldn't have been in the compromising position to begin with."

"I think you're crazy. We *accidentally* got caught in a

rain storm. That's all. No magic," said Charlie. Though there was a little niggle of guilt because rain was predicted that day and she took him fishing at a great distance anyway.

Ian stood. "Believe what you want, little sister-in-law, but I know better." He walked to Rebecca gave her a kiss on the lips and kissed Gracie on the forehead. Then so as not to leave the other children out, he kissed Andy, Freddy and Carrie Ann on the forehead, as well. "I'll see you later. I have to work on the third floor bedrooms today."

After he left, Charlie looked at her sister. "You don't believe that stuff about having to marry the one you love? Do you?"

Rebecca shrugged and took a fussing Gracie from Charlie and put her on her shoulder. "I don't know. Look at Ian and me. We love each other more than either of us thought possible, yet we were forced to marry, which was the best thing to happen to us."

"That's you and Ian. You'd known each other for a quite a while before that happened. Travis and I—"

"Were about to start courting, so you must have liked him, even loved him at that point. I think the same can be said of Travis."

"Becca," said Carrie Ann. "May we be excused."

Charlie looked at their plates.

Rebecca glanced at the empty plates and nodded. "You may. Play in the playroom today. It looks like rain."

She smiled and looked at Charlie. "We wouldn't want you to get caught in it."

Charlie rolled her eyes and shook her head. Then she asked, in all seriousness, "Do you really think Travis is in love with me?"

"Yes, I do." Rebecca kissed each of the children and then each of them kissed Gracie, who giggled.

"I hope you're right, because I think I'm in love with him."

CHAPTER TEN

Charlie walked toward the mercantile for her usual Friday morning shopping trip. All the surrounding farmers and ranchers came in on Saturday and the mercantile was a madhouse so she avoided it. As she passed the alley between the butcher shop and the mercantile she heard a kitten meowing pitifully.

"Hello," she said as she entered the alley. There near a pile of crates was a tiny black kitten. She bent down to see the tiny cat had been tethered to the ground with at thin rope around its back leg.

From behind a higher pile of the crates, a person jumped out and stabbed her in the back. Charlie turned to see her attacker but the person wore an eye mask and covered the lower half of their face with a bandana all beneath a sailor's wool cap.

Charlie went for her gun.

The attacker kicked her in the ribs.

Charlie cried out and fell to her knees, then to the ground.

"Now he'll come to me," the person whispered.

"Lois? Is that you? Why?" Charlie couldn't hear if Lois responded or not. Everything sounded like she was in a tunnel. As she closed her eyes she saw someone in pants running away.

———

"Charlie? Charlie? Can you hear me?"

"Max," she whispered. "The kitten."

"Yes, Max Caldwell. I don't see any kitten. I saw you attacked from across the street at the bank. I'm sorry I didn't catch your assailant, but I need to get you to Doc Wade."

He lifted her.

She groaned. The pain in her back and side was intense but she wasn't dead. *The baby! What about the baby?*

Tears filled her eyes and ran down her cheeks.

"I know it hurts, Charlie, but I'm doing the best I can," said Max.

"No, it's not that. I'm expecting. What about my baby? What if she killed it?"

"The attacker was a woman?"

"I know who attacked me."

"Shh, now. We'll get to that later."

When they reached the doctor's office Max kicked the door with his foot to knock.

Doc opened the door. "Why in tarnation are you kicking my door? Oh, bring her in, quickly." He held the door for Max.

"Follow me, then you better get Travis. He needs to be here."

"Sure thing Doc." Max took her back to the surgery and laid her on the examination table. "You're safe now, Charlie. I'll get Travis and be back shortly."

Charlie closed her eyes. Her side hurt, her shoulder hurt, but she was alive. "Doc. She kicked me in the side. What about the baby?"

Doc Wade leaned over so she could see him. "Don't you worry about that baby. Kicking you in the ribs didn't hurt it. Now, I want you to sit up. I need to examine your ribs and that wound that has you bleeding all over my table."

Though it hurt like heck to move, Charlie sat up with her legs hanging off the side of the table. She gripped her fingers around the edge of the table.

"I need to remove your shirt if I'm to treat that hole in your shoulder. At least it doesn't look like you were shot. Stabbed, were you?"

"Yes." Charlie had trouble breathing. Every breath she took was accompanied by a wave of pain. "And kicked in the side. I think I have broken ribs."

"That could be, but I'm thinking they're just

bruised. You couldn't have sat up on your own if they were broken."

"Good. I'll heal that much sooner."

The door to the room slammed open and Travis rushed through.

"Sweetheart, are you all right?" He ran a hand through his hair. "What am I saying, of course, you're not all right. You're injured. Max said you were attacked." He moved close and reached for her.

"Yes, we'll talk about that at home."

Doc turned to Travis. "You can stay if you keep your mouth shut and step back. I need to sew her up." Doc turned to Charlie. "Stitches will hurt a lot." He walked to a cabinet and pulled a bottle of whiskey and a glass from it pouring two fingers of the brown liquid, he handed to her. "Drink it down. I don't care if you like the taste, I want you to drink it all quickly. I want to give it as much time as possible to start relaxing you and help with the pain when I sew you up. But first, I'll clean the wound."

She took a deep breath and downed the spirits. Charlie couldn't believe people actually drank that stuff on purpose. The liquid burned and she coughed, sure she'd vomit the liquor, but it stayed down.

From the cupboard next to the whiskey, Doc pulled another bottle, this one of witch hazel to clean the injury.

"Travis, come now and hold her."

When Travis was in place with his hands gripping

her upper arms, Doc poured the witch hazel into the wound.

———————

Charlie screamed and fainted against Travis.

"Good. Just hold her still and pray she stays unconscious while I sew her up and wrap her ribs."

"Wrap her ribs?" His gut clenched seeing her injuries. "What the heck happened to her?"

Doc worked quickly and put eight stitches in her right shoulder. "Well, obviously she's been stabbed, but she said the person also kicked her in the ribs. She thinks she has one or more broken ribs." He went back to the counter and this time took cloth from the cabinet underneath the counter. "I'm fairly certain they're only bruised, but the treatment is the same. Her ribcage must be wrapped so the ribs don't move. That'll keep her more comfortable. You can hold her arms up while I wrap her."

Travis did as asked and held her arms straight up while Doc wrapped long strips of cloth around her ribs.

"There that should do it. She should be grateful she was unconscious for the process."

He held her with an arm around her shoulders. "I'm sure when she wakes up she will be. How long will she be out?"

"She should start waking any time now. I'll get this sling on her while she's still out. That will help to keep the shoulder immobile." He placed her right arm in a sling.

"Should I be worried if she's unconscious for longer than an hour or so?"

"No, as a matter of fact I'll wake her now."

The doctor uncapped a small bottle and waved it under Charlie's nose.

She moved her head back and forth, away from the bottle, before opening her eyes.

"Get that stuff away from me."

She reached up to push it away. "Oww. I forgot she stabbed me."

"She?" asked Travis.

"You know who did this to you? Max said he saw what looked like a man running away from the alley. He was wearing pants and a sheepskin coat."

Charlie nodded. "Yes, I saw her, but she spoke to me. I think she thought she'd killed me. She said "Now he'll come to me." It was Lois. I know the attacker was her. I recognized her voice."

Travis' eyes shot wide. "What? That doesn't make sense. I'll talk to her and regardless of what you say, I'm dissolving the association. I want her out of our lives. I should have done it before I ever left Philadelphia."

With her left hand she reached up and touched his chest. "Be careful. I think she's become unhinged since we got married. Maybe before that."

"I don't want you to go anywhere alone. I'll go with you or you'll wait until I can accompany you."

Charlie shook her head. "We can't let her control our lives. I'll simply be more cautious. I won't be checking out any kitten's in alleys I can tell you that. As a matter of fact, I think I'll walk in the street instead of the boardwalk, unless there's a lot of mud."

Travis clenched his fists. "Charlie, you're not thinking straight. You've been gravely injured. Please, do as I ask. You're the one who said she's crazy, let me handle this before you start going anywhere alone."

She pursed her lips. "Since I'll be laid up for a while anyway, I guess it doesn't matter. I won't be leaving the house while I'm wearing a sling."

"That's right," said Doc. "I want you to take it easy for the next ten days. I'll take the stitches out then and you can begin to use the arm."

"Okay. I'll do my best."

Travis let out a long breath and unclenched his fists, happy with her agreement.

Doc crossed his arms over his chest. "I'm very serious about this, Charlie. If you tear those stitches repairing them will be much more difficult...and painful and keep you from using that arm for a longer period of time."

"I hear you, Doc. I'll be good and take it easy but that doesn't mean I'll be in bed for ten days."

"I'm not asking you to be in bed, you're definitely ambulatory, but don't try to lift things where you need both hands. If you cook, do it one-handed. You know what I'm saying."

"Yes, sir, I do and I will."

Doc turned to Travis. "You're my witness. She said she'd follow my instructions and take it easy. She said she would. You heard."

"I did and I'll be making sure she sticks to those words. Right after I take care of another little problem."

Charlie's head shot up and she stared at her husband. "At least wait until I'm not wounded before you give her the boot. I need both arms to defend myself."

"I'll take care of you. You won't be going anywhere she can reach you."

"Oh, really? Are you planning on staying home with me all day long for ten days or longer...until I can use my weapons again?"

Travis cupped his chin with his fingers and stroked a nonexistent beard. "I guess I should just cancel all my appointments and—"

"No, you won't. Those people need you and some of them have been waiting for a long time to get in to see you. You'll keep every appointment and leave well enough alone with Lois." She put two fingers on his lips. "Shh. You'll lose, you might as well admit, I'm right, counselor. It's my word against hers. The marshal can't even do anything yet. But, we should tell him what we know. I agree with that."

Travis frowned and narrowed his eyes. "We have to establish a precedent and tell the marshal what we know. I can do that without you. You don't even need to come with me. It's just a report of what happened and what you know."

Charlie laughed. "All right. You know, you won't win all our arguments. I expect us to fight about things that are important to us and the one they are the most important to will win the day. But this is important to me. I don't want to be attacked when I'm an invalid."

He reached out and smoothed her hair. "You're not an invalid."

"But I feel like one with only one usable arm."

"Do you two mind taking this argument elsewhere? I have patients I need to see," said Doc. "And Charlie I want you to rest as much as possible."

Charlie looked up. "Oh, sorry Doc."

Travis reached in his pocket. "How much do I owe you, Doc? And can I get something for the pain to take home."

Doc went to a cupboard and returned with a small bottle of yellow liquid. "Two dollars. Standard fee for sewing up someone who's been stabbed." Doc chuckled at his joke.

Charlie did not.

Nor did Travis. "Here you go. Thanks very much." He took the bottle and put it in his pocket.

Charlie tried to jump down, with her good hand on the table. "Oww, oh gosh that hurts."

"Move slowly, sweetheart. Healing and moving normally will take a while."

"I guess so." She worked her way off the table and walked out with Travis behind her. As soon as they reached the outside, he took her left arm and tucked her hand in the crook of his elbow.

"With me in a sling, you're making quite the spectacle of us," she griped.

"Hush. No one thinks twice about seeing a man and his wife walking home. They are less likely to stop us and ask questions if they don't notice us in the first place."

"Okay. Sorry. I'm a bit on edge."

"Understandable. You've been traumatized."

"Yeah, next time this happens—"

He shook his head. "There will be no next time."

Charlie huffed out a breath. "Fine. The next time I need stitches, you tell Doc no witch hazel. That stuff nearly killed me."

Travis lifted an eyebrow and patted her hand where it emerged from the crook in his arm. "Actually, it saved you a lot of pain. You might have passed out because of the alcohol but you didn't feel the pain from him stitching you up or when he wrapped your ribs tightly with cloth."

"I knew he'd done something. I can hardly breathe and I didn't think you'd put a corset on me while I was out."

Travis chuckled. His feisty little wife had a wicked sense of humor, and he liked it very much.

———

They reached home without so much as a nod in their direction. As a matter of fact, Charlie thought people were going out of their way not to say something to her about her sling.

"I'm glad we're home. I think that little walk made me tired. I want to rest, and that shouldn't be the case. I used to walk back and forth to town from the house, that's over two miles round trip, without even getting winded. Now I feel like it will be a struggle to go up stairs."

Travis bent down and swept her into his arms. "Then I'll carry you to bed. I don't want you to overly tire yourself." He spoke as he climbed the stairs to their bedroom. "You've been through surgery. Even if you don't remember it, your body does."

He stopped by the bed and set her beside it so he could fluff the pillows. When she laid down he put them behind her so she was sitting up just a bit.

"Do you want the pillows like this or are you ready to sleep?"

"Like this. I'll just rest I think. If I fall asleep that's a bonus."

"Yes, and you need that bonus. I'm a firm believer

that sleep is the best thing you can do for your recovery."

"Well, for right now, I'll agree with you because that's the way my body appears to be going."

He leaned down and kissed her. "Rest now, sweetheart. I'll come check on you a little later." Then he walked out.

She was so tired and closed her eyes.

Suddenly her eyes opened wide.

Sweetheart! He called me sweetheart. What the heck does that mean?

Then she remembered he'd used the endearment in the doctor's office, too. What did he mean? Could he finally realize his feelings for her? Could he be in love with her?

CHAPTER ELEVEN

The day after the incident, Marshal Robert McCauley came to see her.

She greeted him in the living room. "Hi, Robert. Please come sit." She waved toward the green over-stuffed chairs across from the floral printed sofa.

Travis was beside her and held out a hand. "Thanks for coming, Robert. I don't want her going out yet."

"Understandable," said the tall man, with brown hair. He handed Travis a casserole pan covered with oiled cloth and then removed his coat and hat.

Charlie saw he needed a haircut. His hair was about an inch past his shoulders and beginning to curl. "How is Bella?"

"Cooking up a storm. She plans on bringing by more food a little later, since you are injured. Speaking of which, I'm here to talk to you about your attack. Did you see who attacked you?"

"No, I didn't see the person."

"Max said you thought it was Lois Lattimer. How can that be, if you didn't see her?"

Charlie leaned forward from where she sat on the sofa. Her ribs hurt and she winced. "I heard her. She said, "Now he'll come to me." I'm telling you it was Lois."

"That's not enough to go by. I can't arrest her because you thought you heard her—"

She sat back against the cushions of the sofa. "But I—"

Robert held up a hand. "I know you thought you heard her, but if you couldn't see her, you could have imagined that it was her that spoke to you. Heck Charlie, you could have imagined the whole thing and the person didn't speak to you at all. Second, if it was Lois, it'll be her word against yours unless you can find someone who saw her and recognized her."

"What about the scars on my face? She did that to me."

"Can anyone corroborate that statement?"

She blew out a long breath and closed her eyes against the pain in her chest. Then shook her head. "Travis saw me after the fact."

"That's right." Travis patted Charlie's leg. "I can submit a sworn statement to that fact."

Charlie sighed and covered Travis' hand on her leg with her left hand. "Max was the only one who saw anything when she stabbed me. All he saw was someone in a coat and pants running away. For all he knows it was a man."

The marshal leaned forward and rested his elbows on his knees. "For all you know, it was a man and he didn't speak at all. That's the way she would present it, as though the pain from the wound made you imagine her speaking to you. A jury would probably believe her and that's assuming you can get a judge to issue a warrant for her arrest, because as it stands now, I don't have enough to go on to arrest her."

The marshal stood. "I'm sorry as I can be, Charlie, but my hands are tied."

Charlie pushed off using Travis' leg and stood, too. "Don't worry about it Robert. I figured that would be the case, so I'm not surprised." She held out her left hand to him. "Thank you for coming by. Tell Bella I'm looking forward to more of that great French food she prepares."

Robert chuckled. "I think she was delighted you were laid up, not that she wants you injured, but it gives her an excuse to cook all day."

Travis extended his hand to the law man. "You tell Bella she can cook for us anytime. Neither Charlie nor I are any good in the kitchen."

"I'll do that." He opened the door to leave. "You folks, take care."

"You too, Robert," said Charlie, unable to hide her disappointment at the outcome of the interview.

"You, too." Travis closed the door behind the man as he left. "I'm sorry, sweetheart."

There he goes again using that word. He must not mean it the way I do. I use it only for someone I love, but I think he must use it as just something to call me.

"That's no more or less than what you told me to expect. That it would be her word against mine. Let's forget about it and see what kind of good food Bella sent."

———

By the fifth day of her recovery and confinement Charlie was restless and she wanted answers. She knocked and immediately entered Travis' home office.

"I'm bored. Please take me shopping."

He looked up, leaned forward and crossed his hands on top of the desk. "I went to the mercantile and the butcher yesterday."

"Then walk me back to the house so I can visit with Rebecca."

"I'll take you in the buggy but not walking. It's too dangerous."

She put her good hand in her pocket. "It's not my fault that Lois has disappeared, yet I seem to be the one being punished for it." She turned and left the room.

Travis hurried after her. "Wait. Charlie. Wait."

She stopped but didn't turn around.

He walked until he stood in front of her and then clasped her lightly on her upper arms.

"This restriction isn't about punishing you. I want you to be safe and if you go walking about you're not safe."

"You'd be with me. She wouldn't dare to try anything with you there."

He pursed his lips and furrowed his brows. "I don't know—"

She got on tip toe and whispered against his lips. "Please." Then she kissed him. "I need the fresh air and the exercise."

Travis wrapped his arms around her waist and brought her as close as he could without hurting her arm. "You play dirty." Then he took her lips with his. The kiss was deep and hungry.

She returned his kiss with a fervor of her own. Then she pulled back and looked up at him. "Still say *no*?"

He rubbed her nose with his. "I'm thinking about it."

She grinned and kissed him again.

"How about now?"

"Closer."

Charlie giggled at their game and kissed him again. "Now."

"Now, I'll walk you up to see Rebecca."

She kissed him again, long and slow, with the love she felt in her heart. "Thank you. I do appreciate it."

"And what if you get tired?"

"I can take a nap...we can take a nap...in my old room."

He slowly shook his head but his lips formed a small smile.

She knew she'd won and bussed his cheek. "I need to change clothes."

"You look fine."

"I want to wear a dress. After the debacle at the dance, Rebecca made me a new one that's longer to accommodate my boots. And I won't wear my guns either. I'll look like a normal wife out on a stroll with her husband. You said that no one would pay attention to us."

He chuckled. "I did say that didn't I? Well, go change and be careful of your shoulder. Don't strain it."

"I won't," she called over her shoulder, already halfway out the door.

———

Charlie forgot to take into account the fact that except for the dance no one had seen her in a dress. Her shawl hid the sling and she heard lots of ouu's and ahh's. A few of the younger women came up to her.

"Charlie, you look wonderful," said Clara Brewster, an older widow who lived near them in town.

"She does, doesn't she," said Travis.

"I'm so glad you've decided to wear the appropriate garments," said Reverend Trowbridge.

Charlie didn't have the heart to tell him it was only for today.

"You look great, my friend," said Rachel Trowbridge. "I was under the impression you would never again put on a dress." She fell into step along side them.

Charlie noticed Rachel was carrying a man's shirt that looked familiar. "Is that Ben's?"

Rachel's color rose and she ducked her head. "Yes, he asked if I could sew the button on the cuff. He said Rebecca didn't have time with Gracie and the little children to keep under control."

Charlie lifted her eyebrows. "Really. That's most interesting."

"Yes, he said Rebecca didn't want to ask you because she knows how much you hate mending."

"That's true enough."

They walked along in silence until they approached the house.

"Is there something between you and Ben?" asked Charlie.

Rachel shrugged. "I don't honestly know. He acts like he wants to court me one minute and pulls away the next."

Charlie put her left hand on Rachel's shoulder. "That's because he was wounded, heck he was shattered, by his last courtship. They had been sweethearts since grade school. Everyone knew they would marry and the date was set. The church was filled to the rafters with our friends and neighbors. We waited and waited for *her* to show up. Finally, a messenger came into the church and handed Ben a piece of paper. His fiancé had run off with someone else."

Rachel's eyes widened. "Who was she?"

Charlie leaned over and whispered. "I don't even say her name anymore. I'm afraid I'll invoke the devil."

Rachel laughed a little and then noticed that Charlie did not.

Her eyes narrowed and her brows furrowed. "You're serious."

Charlie shrugged. "Maybe not the actual devil, but bad things will happen and I don't take the chance. Besides it riles up Ben and I don't want to do that to him."

The woman nodded. "No, of course, you wouldn't."

Charlie laughed. "I wouldn't go as far as to say that, but I try not to hurt my brothers and sisters on purpose."

Travis held the gate open for the ladies first and he followed behind.

Rachel placed a hand on Charlie's left shoulder. You're a good sister."

"Why didn't you say anything about my arm being in a sling?"

Rachel shrugged. "I figured you'd tell me if you wanted me to know."

"I was stabbed...by Travis' business assistant, Lois Lattimer."

Rachel's hand flew to cover her mouth as she sucked

in a breath. "I'd heard you were injured because Miranda saw you come out of Doc's office in the sling, but other than that I had no idea. How horrible!"

"It's better now, but I needed to get out of the house. Visiting with Rebecca, even if I can't hold Gracie, will be nice."

"Yes, it will. That little niece of yours is a heart breaker and she's not even a year old yet."

"I know. The boys had better watch out when she gets to school. I won't have my niece being taken advantage of for any reason. If she can't handle them Auntie Charlie can." Her hand automatically went to where her left holster would be.

They climbed the stairs to the porch and saw Rebecca outside with her coat on and Gracie wrapped in blankets. She sat in the swing and had it slowly moving.

Rachel waved at Rebecca and continued on into the house.

Rebecca nodded back at Rachel.

Charlie and Travis walked over to Rebecca. She sat next to her sister and niece. "Gracie, having trouble sleeping?"

Travis leaned against the porch railing.

"Yes, and I've tried everything else, so we're trying this and it seems to be working. At least she's not screaming at the top of her lungs."

"Do you think she's teething? Remember when Carrie Ann went through this stage?" The baby was lying on her tummy on Rebecca's lap while she swung very slowly. The motion seemed to soothe the baby.

"I do, but I think she has a stomach ache this time. What are you doing here? Travis said Doc said to rest for ten days."

"I couldn't take it anymore. I was going absolutely crazy. So I begged—"

"Cajoled and bribed," said Travis with a grin.

Charlie rolled her eyes at her husband.

"I suppose you just kissed him a few times." Rebecca smiled a knowing smile.

"Yes. Is it just him and Ian that like to be kissed so much?"

"I'll answer that," said Ian as he came out of the house and joined them on the porch. "It is not just me and Travis. All men love to be kissed whether by our wives or our baby daughters." He bent down and Rebecca gave him a kiss and then he opened the blanket and kissed the back of Gracie's head. "See?"

Charlie and Rebecca both shook their heads, but they also chuckled.

Ian smoothed the hair on his daughters head. "Is she feeling any better?"

Rebecca looked down at Gracie. "She seems to be. I'm taking her inside. I don't want her to catch cold, just wanted a bit of fresh air." She put the baby on her shoulder and covered her with the blanket head to toe, and then she stood. "Let's go in now."

She walked into the house, and the rest of them followed.

Travis put an arm around Charlie.

She leaned into him and laid a hand on her stomach thinking about the baby she carried. *Will I know what to do if he or she gets sick? I guess I'm lucky I can ask Rebecca or Max's wife, Lydia. Between the two of them they've probably had to face all of the problems with babies.*

As if he knew what she was thinking, Travis squeezed her shoulders lightly so as not to hurt her. "You'll do fine...*we'll* do fine...as parents. Remember Rebecca wasn't a mother before Gracie."

"Not true. Rebecca raised Carrie Ann from the day she was born. I wasn't in the family house, until Father died. Then I came home. Carrie Ann was already one by that time. Gracie is the first newborn I've been around."

"But even at one year, Carrie Ann was still a baby, so you have experience. You'll be a great mother. Trust me."

She looked up at him, her heart nearly bursting with love. "I do trust you. That in itself is amazing. I don't give my trust easily, but if I can't trust my husband, then who can I trust?"

Travis moved his hand up to the place where her neck met her shoulder and pulled her to him, while he bent down and placed his lips on hers. When he pulled back he laid his forehead on hers. "I never tire hearing that phrase and with you I never know what to expect."

"Good. You'll always be on your toes that way."

He shook his head and grinned. Then he lowered his hand to her waist and they walked into the kitchen.

Rebecca and Ian sat at the table with her holding Gracie.

As they entered the kitchen, she looked up. "I was beginning to wonder if you two would ever come in here. Sit and have some coffee and tell me what's on your mind."

Charlie shrugged. "Oww." She looked over her shoulder at her wound. "Shouldn't the darn thing have quit hurting by now?"

Travis rolled his eyes and then at Rebecca. "Will you tell her she was severely injured and the wound will not heal quickly? She doesn't seem to believe me or Doc."

Charlie frowned. "Will you pour us some coffee and quit telling stories on me, please?"

Travis chuckled and walked to the cupboard to get cups. He brought them each a cup and then sat next to Charlie.

"So what really brings you two up this way?" asked Ian.

Gracie began to fuss.

Ian reached for her. "Here let me have her. Maybe she just needs some Daddy time." He took the infant and put her up to his shoulder, holding her with one arm under her bum and the other behind her head. "There we go, baby girl. You're fine. Daddy's got you."

Rebecca smiled. "He's so good with her and she

adores him. Watch, she'll probably settle down just at the sound of his voice."

Gracie sniffled and laid her head on her father's shoulder.

Ian hummed.

In not too many minutes Gracie slept...content...in her daddy's arms.

She waved a hand toward the two. "See what I mean? I've been trying for hours to get her to sleep and she fights me every time. I finally give up and let Ian have her and she falls right to sleep."

Charlie laughed quietly, so as not to wake the baby. "She just finds Ian boring."

He narrowed his eyes. "Laugh now, but you'll be doing the same thing come November."

"Okay." She held up her hands. "You're right. Truce. I won't insult your parenting if you stop reminding me of the bad things that go along with being a mother."

Ian smiled. "Deal."

Rebecca slapped her husband on the arm and turned to her sister. "Being a mother isn't all crying babies, you know that. You had Carrie Ann giggling all the time when she was a baby. You'll be fine."

She sighed. "That's what Travis keeps telling me."

He nodded. "Yes, I do. I think she'll be a great mother."

Rebecca cocked her head. "So listen to him. You *will* be a fine mama."

Charlie frowned. "But how do you know? How can anyone know what kind of parent they'll be?"

"Because I know you will love this baby wilh all your heart and that's what convinces me," said Rebecca.

Charlie placed her hand on her stomach. "Yes, I will. I already do."

Rebecca tilted her head and her eyes teared over. "I know you do. You couldn't do anything else being who you are."

"I hope you're right. I want to be a good mother. I want to be like you."

CHAPTER TWELVE

Charlie got her stitches out and began to use her right arm, stretching it, making circles and whatever she could do to get the movement back. Ten days didn't seem like much time to lose the motion, but it was ten days in a sling.

She tried drawing her pistol and was slow. She'd never been a fast draw, but she was way too slow now. She needed to practice. Their house was on the edge of town with nothing behind it, so she set up some cans and practiced until she was comfortable drawing her weapon.

Gathering the cans in a burlap bag she headed back to the house.

"Did you get your motion back? Guess I didn't go deep enough. You were supposed to die."

Charlie pulled her weapon, dropped the bag with a clatter and swung around to face Lois. "You're taking your life in your hands sneaking up on me like that. I might have killed you. I still might."

Standing between Charlie and the house, she shook her head, and the sun glinted off her black hair. "I don't think you will. You're too honorable to shoot an unarmed woman."

"I am." She holstered her weapon.

Lois pulled a derringer from her pocket. "You and I are going for a walk."

"Too bad for me you don't have the same morals. I don't think we're going anywhere and I thought you said you were unarmed. Must be a new acquisition. You didn't use it on me before, so you must have bought it since."

Lois laughed. "I did and I lied. That shouldn't surprise you, though by your reaction I can see that it does."

Suddenly Charlie charged Lois angling to the right.

The woman's eyes widened and she pointed the gun back and forth at Charlie who zigged and zagged as she ran.

Lois fired.

The bullet grazed Charlie's arm but not enough to slow her as she tackled Lois.

They rolled around on the grass in the meadow, each trying to get the upper hand. With each roll, Charlie's sides ached, but she wouldn't let up. Couldn't let Lois get the upper hand.

Charlie finally reared back and slammed her fist into Lois' jaw.

The woman fell to the ground unconscious.

Charlie took a moment to catch her breath then took the knife from her boot and cut two long strips from Lois' skirt. She tied the woman's hands and then her ankles. Lois wouldn't be going anywhere soon.

Getting to her feet, Charlie dusted herself off, took one last look at Lois and went to get the marshal.

———

She opened the door and entered the marshal's office. "Robert, I have her."

He sat behind his desk going through wanted posters. "You have who? Lois? Why?"

"She pulled a gun on me and tried to kill me. She shot at me and hit me in the arm." She turned so he could see the bloody sleeve of her shirt. "I knocked her out and tied her up. Now you have to come get her. She's behind my house."

He stood and grabbed his hat. "All right, let's go."

Together, they walked the two blocks to Charlie and Travis' house and then to the meadow behind it.

"She's right there," Charlie pointed to a place on the ground surrounded by tall grass. An empty place on the ground. "What in the——? She was right here." Charlie bent down and picked up the piece of material she tied around her ankles. It had been cut. "She had a knife. Somewhere, she had a knife. I knew I should have checked her body, but I was in too much of a hurry to get you." Charlie was disappointed in herself. She should not have been in such a hurry, should have checked her body, should have done so many things different.

"Well, seeing your wound and the cut material from her dress, I have enough to arrest her on. If I had the derringer, I would for sure."

"Well, she dropped it when I tackled her. Maybe it's still around here. Help me look."

Robert and Charlie combed the area. Charlie was just about to give up when she saw something glint in the sunlight.

"Robert. I found it." She bent and picked up the small weapon carrying it to the marshal.

The first thing he did was check the chamber.

"Just as you said, it's definitely been fired." He looked up at her. "You need to go see Doc about that wound on your arm."

She nodded, reached over, touched her arm and grimaced. "Now I can. You have the gun and enough to arrest her, if she shows her face around here again. Somehow, I think that is doubtful. She knows she's been caught now."

"Never underestimate your opponent. She still hasn't achieved her objective which is to kill you. I believe she'll try again and this time there won't be any stopping her until one of you is dead. Keep on your toes, Charlie. She'll be back. Take my word for it."

Gratified he was taking the situation seriously, she nodded. "Oh, I do. I'll be more prepared and won't let her get the drop on me again, I guarantee that. I just might shoot and ask questions later."

Robert frowned. "I don't recommend that action either. You could go to jail for that action, especially if you kill her. Just let me do my job. I promise I'll handle it."

Charlie shrugged. "All right. I'll let you do your job, but you better hope she doesn't come after me again. I won't be responsible for anything but protecting myself."

"I understand and I expect you to protect yourself, that's only reasonable."

She looked at her arm. "I better go see Doc. My arm is starting to hurt some."

He lifted his eyebrows and nodded. "I imagine it is. It's more than a scratch as the doctor will tell you."

"Yeah, he'll probably holler at me, as will Travis when he finds out."

"I would suggest that after you see the doctor, you go see Travis, either that or you get my wife to cook you a special dinner for tonight."

Charlie brightened. "Do you think Bella would?"

The marshal cocked an eyebrow and crossed his arms over his chest. "No, she will not. I was only kidding. You need to talk to Travis."

Dread filled her and her stomach was suddenly in knots. "You're right. I know you are, but that doesn't mean I'm looking forward to it."

"He wants you safe more than anything. He'll remember that after he gets done being upset. Trust me."

She started walking away. "I know. Talk to you later, Robert." She waved over her shoulder.

———

At the doctor's office, Charlie got the reaction she expected from Doc Wade. First he scolded her for not coming in immediately, then he patched her up.

Doc frowned while he stitched Charlie's wound closed. "This woman, Lois, seems to have an unusual interest in eliminating you from this earth. This is the second time she's sent you to me bleeding. Perhaps you should avoid her."

"Do you think I'm not trying? She attacks me when I'm not expecting it, jumping out at me from alleys and pulling a gun on me when she is supposed to be unarmed."

"She made a nice groove in your arm that I'll sew up. It's small enough I don't see why the wound would restrict your movement any. I suggest you continue your practice...and next time protect yourself."

"Don't worry, Doc. I've kind of worked that out for myself."

"Well, good because the next time I see you, I don't want to have to stitch you up anywhere. I want to see how you're doing with your pregnancy. This kind of stress is not good for you or the baby."

She let out a slow breath to control the pain from the throbbing of the wound on her arm. "I understand totally, Doc and that's the only thing I want to see you for, as well. Do you think I like being shot? Trust me, I don't."

"Okay, then. You're all set. I'll see you next month unless you feel there is something wrong with the baby."

"I hear you. I'll be careful." She laid a protective hand on her stomach.

She paid her bill and trudged out of the doctor's office, not looking forward to relating the latest trouble to her husband.

———

She walked to the house they had bought for 'Travis' office and upon entering smiled at his new secretary, Nadine Grimm. The pretty young woman had vibrant red hair and the personality to go with it.

"Hi Nadine. Is he in?"

"He's always in for you. Go on back. He doesn't have anyone with him right now. But he's got an appointment in about ten minutes."

"Okay, I'll try to hurry."

Nadine shook her head and waved an arm forward. "Don't worry about it. I'll try to make the old blister wait until you're done."

"Who's coming in?"

"Old Mrs. Orndoor. She says she wants her neighbor arrested and then insults the marshal at the same time. Even with your sweet disposition, you'd call her an old blister."

"Tell you what. I'll go in and see him, but when Mrs. Orndoor shows up, you interrupt and then show her in, or better yet, just send her back."

"Oh, trust me, she'll go back on her own. She won't care what I say or that he has someone else with him."

"Good. I guess I best go see him now. Talk to you later, Nadine. Thanks."

———

Charlie strolled into Travis' office like she had all the time in the world.

He looked up and smiled. "Well, what brings my lovely wife to see me today?"

"Well, I have some news that I didn't want to wait until dinner to tell you."

"Come sit and tell me what couldn't wait."

She licked her lips which seemed overly dry for some reason. "There is no easy way to say this...I got shot today. Nothing critical, just a crease in my arm the doctor had to sew up,"

Travis shot to his feet and came around the desk. "Shot?!"

Charlie told him about her eventful morning.

"Look. It wasn't—"

"I'm going in, I don't care who's with him. He'll see me."

Charlie turned toward the voice. An old woman on the larger side, with white hair and using a cane entered the room.

"Time to leave, Charlie. You can talk to him at home, I can't." She waved her cane toward the door.

"Yes ma'am. I wouldn't want to intrude on your appointment." She turned to Travis. "I'll see you later."

He started to follow her. "Charlie, wait we'll talk after—"

Mrs. Orndoor held up her cane and placed it against his chest. "Oh, no you don't. You have an appointment with me and you'll keep it, young man. You can talk to your wife at home."

Frowning, Travis pushed down the cane.

Charlie slipped from the room and hurried out the door.

Nadine was nowhere to be seen.

Since Charlie figured she was fairly safe from Lois, she went to the butcher and picked up a pork roast, Travis' favorite. Then she went to the mercantile, bought a couple of potatoes, and the makings for an apple pie.

She kept her wits about her on the way to and from the stores and saw no sign of Lois.

After putting away all her purchases, she prepared the roast and placed it in the oven. Then she made the pie and left it on the counter until the oven was free.

Checking around the kitchen she decided all was prepared as much as she could do right this minute and headed upstairs to change before he came home. She had no doubt that he would be there as soon as he could get Mrs. Orndoor out of his office, which she hoped was a long time from now.

She had just stepped out of the kitchen when she heard the front door open.

"Charlie!"

She didn't like the sound of his tone. If she hurried she could make it out the back door—

"Charlie, don't even think it." He pointed at her.

She could tell by his voice and his narrowed eyes that he was not happy.

She walked away from the door. "I was just going to let you calm down."

"You think avoiding me will make me calm down? All that will do is make me angrier when I do finally talk to you." He stalked toward her.

She backed up until she hit the counter with her bottom.

He took her by the shoulders and then ran his hands down her arms.

"Oww!" She opened her eyes wide.

He quickly lifted his hands away from her. "Is that where she shot you? I'm so sorry. I didn't mean to hurt you."

"You didn't? But you're angry with me and you're a man. I'm a woman and I'm supposed to obey but I—"

He placed two fingers over her lips. "Charlie, I don't expect you to blindly obey me. I expect you to talk to me about the problem and let us find a solution together. Yes, I may get angry, but I'll never hit you no matter how angry I get."

She couldn't really believe her ears. "You won't? And you haven't, but my father—"

"Your father was a monster if he beat you children. I don't care what you did to make him angry. He was the adult, not the child, and should have acted like one. I'm so sorry you had to endure that. I think I understand you better now that I know."

He reached up and wiped a tear from her cheek.

She didn't realize she was crying. Then she threw her arms around his neck and bawled.

He wrapped his arms around her waist and brought her close.

What else would she discover with Travis that was totally unlike her father, the man who shaped her into the person she was?

CHAPTER THIRTEEN

Lois paced the inside of the little cabin she'd found in the woods outside of town. It appeared to be abandoned, which was very good for her. Whoever lived there left not long ago. Though the pegs for clothes in the bedroom were empty, the bed was still there and she found a blanket that had been forgotten on the side of the bed next to the wall. At least, she could stay warm.

She was a fully capable woman, able to get her own kindling and use the firewood someone before her cut.

A couple of cans of vegetables remained in the kitchen area but all she had to open them with was her knife and it wouldn't work well. That was all right. She could go for a day or two before she needed to eat. Long enough to let things die down. Then she'd break in to the home of the butcher or baker, or someone else who was gone all day. Perhaps the owner of the mercantile, Ernest Duncanson, would be better. She knew for a fact that he, his wife and two sons, all worked in the store every day. Saturday, tomorrow, would be the best day to break in. All of them would definitely be working on the busiest day of the week.

With her plans made Lois stoked the fire and got the blanket from the bedroom. She moved the old rocker in front of the fire, wrapped up in the blanket and tried to keep warm. Winter was still upon them, and even with the fire the cabin was cold. She'd have to be judicious with the wood, or she'd run out before her plans came together.

Lois wasn't an idiot. She knew Travis would never accept her now. If she'd killed Charlotte the first time and gotten away with it...maybe. But now he knew she was behind the attacks, he'd never forgive her.

She knew he was in love with his wife, even if he didn't. Mourning her, he wouldn't start a new relationship. After all these years, she should know she wasn't his choice, but she would be now.

He would come with her, or she would kill Charlie.

Charlie. It was a man's name. Why would she want to be known by a man's name when Charlotte was so pretty? Not plain like Lois.

She rocked slowly in the chair. But she was anything but plain. Her hair was lustrous, rich and black. Her eyes were the deepest emerald green, all in a pale face with a rosebud mouth and pink cheeks. She was a beautiful woman.

Why couldn't Travis see that? Why couldn't he want her?

———

Charlie managed to get Travis to understand why she did things yesterday in the order she'd done them. She really hadn't had any choice. She needed the marshal to help her, and then needed to see the doctor. When she'd finished with the doctor she went to Travis. The order of things was logical, not emotional, and she was being logical in dealing with Lois.

Her emotional side wanted to run to Travis and cry on his shoulder. Have him hold her and tell her he loved her. But that wouldn't be happening.

He'd warned her. Hadn't he warned her not to fall in love with him?

Hadn't she said that circumstance would never happen? She never wanted to fall in love. People you love hurt you. Hadn't her father, the man she loved most in the world thrown her out into the street when she was seventeen?

Hadn't her mother, left them all? Left her adoring husband with five children including a newborn babe? Turning that adoring husband into a bitter, angry man who'd taken out that anger on his children and then drank himself to death.

Had it mattered that Charlie wasn't prepared for any of that to happen?

Nothing mattered. Love made you hurt. That fact was all that was true in the end. Love made you hurt.

I won't think about that now. I have other fish to fry and kettles to watch. I have a husband who doesn't want to let me out of the house but I won't be caged. I won't go back to having someone else control me and what I do. I can't. I'm not that person.

Charlie headed outside and to the mercantile for flour to make molasses cookies and potatoes to go with the pork chops she had for that night's dinner. They were Travis' favorite. As she was passing by the Duncanson house she noticed movement. Knowing the family all worked at the store, she pulled her gun and went to investigate.

Coming around the side of the house, she saw Lois go inside through the back door. Time to end this. Lois was going to jail. There would be no tying her up and getting the marshal. She would drag her to his office if she had to. Stealthily she slipped to the kitchen window, peeked in and moved away just as fast. The woman was in the kitchen searching in the icebox.

She must be hungry. This would be the only way she could get food. Steal it. Lois was smart. She knew the family would be working today and out of the house. Easy enough to break in, maybe she didn't even have to. Few people locked their doors in Oregon City. It was considered a safe town.

Charlie worked her way around to the front door. She would come in at her from the back. She tiptoed across the porch and tried the doorknob. It turned. Opening the door as quietly as possible, she slipped inside and made her way toward the back of the house where the kitchen was.

Entering the kitchen, she poised her weapon. "Put up your hands, Lois."

There was no response.

Charlie moved farther into the room and looked around. Empty. She hurried to the window and looked out but didn't see anyone. No movement of any kind, even the air was still.

She cussed but didn't holster her gun. Exiting through the kitchen door she heard a scuffle.

"Let me up, you old hag."

That was Lois' voice.

Charlie scooted around the side of the house and saw Mrs. Orndoor, in her pink chenille dressing gown, sitting on Lois' back.

Her face covered in mud, Lois hollered at the top of her lungs.

Food stuffs were scattered everywhere.

Mrs. Orndoor thumped Lois on the head with her cane.

"Stop hitting me with that." She tried to knock the woman off of her by arching her back but the old girl had a good seventy pounds on Lois.

"Mrs. Orndoor. How did you capture her?"

"I saw her go into the Duncansons' and knew she'd be coming out the same way and when she walked by my back porch I jumped on her. I don't have a railing. I keep meaning to put one up, but good thing I hadn't, or this...woman...would have gotten away with stealing from Ernest."

Charlie laughed. "You did a great job. Do you think you can keep her there while I get the marshal?"

"You can't leave me here." Lois yelled. "She's liable to kill me."

Charlie's laughter died. She bent down to speak directly to Lois. "Would serve you right. You're likely to hang anyway for attempted murder, twice."

The woman didn't say anything else.

Mrs. Orndoor hit her again.

"Ow! What was that for?" Lois rubbed her head.

"Just wanted to make sure you were still alive. Can't have you dyin' before the marshal gets here. Of course, that would save him some time, but..." She raised her free hand to her chin and placed two fingers there. "No. I want him to see you." She rapped Lois on the head again.

"Ow! Stop that!" Lois turned her head to the side and put her hands over the top to protect it from the next rap by the cane.

Charlie ran to the marshal's office, making her wound ache, and slammed the door open.

"Robert. Marshal. Come quickly."

Robert immediate stood. "Whoa, Charlie. Where's the fire?"

"Mrs. Orndoor captured Lois Latimer. You've got to see this for yourself."

Robert grabbed his hat and ran with Charlie to the Duncansons'.

Lois and Mrs. Orndoor were where she left them.

Robert burst into laughter. "Now that capture was worth running to see."

The old woman tapped Lois on the head again with her cane.

"You old biddy, when I get out of here, I'm going to make you very sorry you did this."

"Lady, you're not getting out of here," said Robert walking close to the two women. "Here now, let me help you up, Edna. You did a wonderful job here. Thank you."

The old woman actually blushed.

Charlie covered her smile with her fingers.

"Why, thank you marshal." Mrs. Orndoor placed her hand in Robert's and he pulled her to her feet. She stepped over the prone body of Lois.

For her part Lois got to her hands and knees and stopped. "I don't think I can stand on my own."

Robert stepped forward to help her.

Charlie grabbed his arm. "Don't believe her. She's trying to escape. Don't believe a thing she says."

He nodded and stopped. "You'll have to rise on your own or I'll be forced to drag you by your ankles."

Lois snorted and stood. "What's the world coming to that a man doesn't help up a lady anymore?"

"You're not a lady," said Charlie.

Lois turned her muddy face toward Charlie. "Takes a whore to know one."

Charlie fisted her hands and clenched her jaw, but didn't take the bait. "You can call me whatever you like. Everyone here, knows different."

But she wondered. Did everyone know differently? Did they believe that she'd been less than a virgin on her wedding night, since she and Travis married the next day? What is she thinking? Of course, they did. That's why she and Travis had married in the first place, because of what people would think.

She shrugged, releasing some of the tension in her shoulders. What people thought didn't really matter. She'd stopped caring when her father kicked her out. The only people whose opinion she valued was her family's and they knew nothing had happened. So, why had she agreed to the marriage? She told herself it was to protect Travis' reputation, with him starting a new business and all. Somewhere inside that reason might have been true, but she knew she married him because she'd fallen in love with him. Against her own desires she'd fallen and fallen hard for her husband.

———

Charlie strolled over to Travis' office not wanting to tell him what had just happened. She knew he would tell her he was happy about Lois but admonish her for being out on her own.

She entered his office.

His eyes narrowed and he got red in the face as he stood behind his desk. "What are you doing here? You're not supposed to be out of the house. It's not safe."

She sat in the chair in front of his desk. "If you'll let me speak, you'll understand everything."

"Fine. Speak."

She held up a hand and ticked off on her fingers. "First," she put down one finger. "I'm not a dog, don't treat me like one." She was happy to see him blush. At least she hit a nerve. "Second," she put down a second finger. "I don't have to worry about going about on my own. Lois was just captured and taken to jail."

"What? How? Who?"

She told him the story and by the time she finished he was roaring with laughter, his anger at her gone.

He walked around the desk to her, took her hand and helped her to stand. "I'm sorry that I yelled at you. I was just so scared for you. Lois could have been lying in wait, watching the house for all we knew."

She cupped his jaw. "Thank you for worrying about me, but I am perfectly safe now. No one will be sneaking up on me again."

"I'm your husband and allowed to worry. That's part of what husbands do."

Charlie sighed and pulled away. "I've been independent for many years now. I find depending on someone else and having them worry about me...restricting. I must be allowed to be myself. I don't believe I'm who you want me to be."

Travis followed her and wrapped her in his arms. "I want you any way I can have you. I'll do my best to give you the freedom you crave. I don't want to break your spirit, Charlie. I want to take care of you, yes, but I need to learn to do that whether you're in your pants or wearing a dress."

"Are you sure you wouldn't rather find someone you might could love?"

"You're having my child. I would never divorce you and I will never find anyone to love any more than I do you."

That's an interesting way of phrasing that sentence. It could mean he loves me or just that he'll never love anyone. Which way does he mean it?

"As you wish. I was headed to the mercantile when everything happened with Lois. I think I'll continue on my errand. I have a nice pair of pork chops and needed some potatoes. Is there anything else you want from there?"

He shook his head. "Nothing. I'll be home early today."

"Good. You can help me cook."

"Oh, I'll help you." He whispered in her ear.

Charlie gasped. "You wouldn't."

Travis grinned and lifted his brows. "I can and you will, I promise."

She rolled her eyes and shook her head. "You are an ornery man, Travis MacGregor."

"I have to be in order to keep up with my ornery wife."

She grinned, gave him a quick kiss on the cheek then headed out to the mercantile.

All the way there she thought about what Travis had said. Was he saying he loved her?

CHAPTER FOURTEEN

Charlie brought her purchases home and prepared a special dinner for Travis. One of his favorite, pork chops with mashed potatoes and gravy, fresh bread and a cherry pie from the bakery. She wanted tonight to be special. Telling Travis of her love for him would be difficult, but she needed to say the words regardless if he said them back.

Thirty minutes before he was to arrive home, she sauntered upstairs to change her clothes, brush her hair and wash her face and hands.

She put on her one and only dress. It was a good thing Travis liked it on her. When there was time she'd ask Rebecca to make her another one. Or she'd see if anyone had set up shop as a dressmaker. She hadn't heard of one, but that didn't mean a thing. New businesses were popping up all the time as new people came to Oregon City.

Unbraiding her hair she was left with pretty waves. She ran her fingers through to loosen them and then left the thick mass of blonde hair cascading down her back.

Suddenly she heard someone come in and looked at the clock on the bureau..

Travis wasn't due for another fifteen minutes. Had Lois escaped and come for her?

Charlie grabbed one of her pistols and slipped downstairs. Following noises in the kitchen, she burst in, pistol in hand.

Travis was there moving things around in the icebox.

"You're home early. I hadn't expected you." She lowered the pistol to her side.

He straightened and looked her way, eyebrows furrowed. "Why are you greeting me with a gun? Did Lois escape?"

"Not that I'm aware of. Now why are you home early?"

His face softened and he gave her a small smile. "Come and sit, Charlie. I've got something to say to you."

She sat and put her gun on the table beside her. "Okay, what do you want to say?"

He knelt in front of her. "Charlie, will you marry me?"

She frowned. "We're already married?"

He took her hand in his. "I know, but I want this one in front of the whole community. I want everyone to know that I choose you and you choose me...freely. Without needing to but because we love each other."

Charlie's heart stopped and then started beating a rapid tattoo in her chest. She was sure Travis could hear it.

Tears filled her eyes. "You...you love me?"

He smiled. "Yes, I figured you knew by now."

She shook her head as tears ran down her cheeks. "You always said you couldn't...wouldn't ever love me."

"I was a fool. I think I've loved you since you took my dollar and bought candy for the children. How could I not love such a kind, generous woman?"

Charlie cried for a minute and then sniffled.

He rubbed circles in her palm with his thumb. "Charlie, do you think you can find it in your heart to love me, too?"

She closed her eyes, then opened them and blinked several times. "I can. I do. I love you. I was going to tell you over dinner. Dinner!" She stood quickly and ran to the stove, grabbed a couple of dish towels and pulled the pork chops out of the oven where she'd put them to finish cooking. "I think they're fine."

Travis wrapped his arms around her waist and nuzzled the back of her neck. "Can dinner wait? Because I don't think I can. I want to make love, real love, to my wife. The woman I will cherish and love forever."

Charlie turned in his arms, her throat dry. "I'd like

that very much. Very much indeed." She took his hand and led him upstairs.

Dinner was very, very late.

———

One month later

Rebecca helped Charlie into her dress. The gown was pink satin with pearls around the bottom of the high neck and pearl buttons on the cuffs. A wide, red velvet ribbon was tied at her waist with a large bow in back. The low bodice was filled with delicate white lace up to the collar.

Travis had spared no expense on her dress. He wanted her to have exactly what she wanted.

Charlie had dreamed of a dress like this when she was a little girl and like any little girl she dreamed of a big wedding.

She got her wish. The church brimmed with people standing at the back and around the walls of the sanctuary.

Ben walked her down the aisle.

Rebecca stood up with her as her matron of honor.

Ian was Travis' best man.

Reverend Trowbridge beamed as he performed the ceremony.

The ceremony felt different from the first one. Maybe because all of their friends were there but she thought it was probably because she and Travis loved each other this time and knew it.

When the wedding was over, everyone went to the community hall. Their wedding reception was like any other community dance. Every family had supplied food. Rebecca made a special chocolate layer cake with white butter cream frosting—Charlie's favorite.

Travis' and Charlie danced only the first and last dances together. In between she thought she'd danced with every man there twice, but she was so happy she didn't care that her feet hurt.

At about six o'clock everyone dispersed and went home.

Travis and Charlie headed out, as well.

"Do you want to stay at the hotel tonight?" he asked.

She tucked her hand into the crook of his arm and leaned into him. "Nope. I want to be in my own house, where if I decide to walk around naked I can and no one can tell me I can't."

Travis stopped walking and turned to her, lifting her chin. He kissed her gently and then he touched her lips with his tongue.

She opened and then wrapped her arms around his neck.

He pulled back. "I love you, Charlotte MacGregor. I don't believe I'll ever get tired of saying that. I love you."

She smiled. "I will never get tired of hearing you say

the words. Nor will I get tired of saying them to you. I love you, Travis MacGregor, with all my heart."

She took his arm again and they walked home, rushed up the stairs.

He kept his word and kept her in bed all weekend making love, talking and making love again.

As far as Charlie was concerned, it was the perfect honeymoon.

Five years later

Charlie sat on the sofa in the living room and bounced Travis Jr. on her knee. She'd had him in her arms since after dinner. But the six-month-old was teething and nothing seemed to make him happy. He leaned back, stiffened and then tried to throw himself off her lap.

"Oh, baby, I'm so sorry, I know your mouth hurts." She gave him a sugar tit to suck on and that quieted him for a while.

Becca galloped into the room on her stick pony, her puppy, Rover, yapping at her heels. She was wearing her pants and the little boots her daddy had bought her.

"Whoa there, Buttercup. Where are you going galloping through here so fast?"

"Daddy's behind me. He's gonna catch me. I gotta go."

She watched her four-year-old race away just as her father, riding his own stick horse galloped in.

"Whoa, there Jasper." He pulled the stick horse to a halt in front of her, set the horse on the carpet and gave her a quick kiss on the lips before sitting next to her. "Your daughter is about to wear out her poor father." He panted as he caught his breath. "She's had me racing around outside for the last twenty minutes."

"Would you rather have Trav? He's teething and not very happy."

He looked at his son. "He's happy now."

She jutted her chin. "Just until he gets tired of the sugar tit."

He laughed and shook his head. "I'll stick with little Miss Buttercup. Hopefully, she won't realize I'm not behind her for a while."

Charlie chuckled. "Getting old, Daddy?"

He nodded, eyes wide. "When it comes to our exuberant daughter, I think so. Where does she get all her energy? Were you like this as a child?"

She shrugged. "I have no idea, but Carrie Ann was when she was four. She kept all of us busy. We took her in shifts, Ben, Rebecca and I. Peter was just a kid himself, so he didn't have to watch her except for very rare occasions, at least before I left home."

His gaze narrowed and his fist clenched. "I'm still angry at your father for the way he treated you. Fathers are supposed to love and support their children. Help them grow into good adults. At least you came out well."

"You can thank my mama for that before she passed on. As for Becca, I'm not letting her cut her hair. Carrie Ann may have been allowed to do that, but I didn't have any say in that decision. I do with Becca. I know I should let her be more independent, but there are just some things I insist on until she gets old enough to know her mind."

Travis raised his hands in front of him. "You won't find me disagreeing. I don't want her to cut her hair either. I suppose she can if she wants, when she's an adult but I hope she doesn't."

Travis Jr. was asleep in his mother's arms.

"I'm afraid to move that he might wake up, but I need to put him in his crib. He'll sleep better and longer."

"Here, let me have him."

Travis stood and reached for the sleeping baby.

Charlie lifted the infant into his father's arms.

They walked upstairs together.

Travis didn't need to lower the side of the crib to put the baby down. At six-foot-four he was tall enough to just lean over and place little Travis on the mattress.

"He didn't wake," whispered Charlie, with relief as she leaned into her husband's side.

He put his arm around her and kissed the top of her head. "That's because I'm good at this. Though I think our daughter will send me to an early grave."

She looked up at him, her eyes narrowed. "Don't even talk like that. You're barely thirty-five. You're not dying anytime soon. I won't allow it."

He laughed. "I love you, Charlotte MacGregor."

She smiled before putting her arms around his neck and kissing him hard. The kiss was very hungry. "I love you, too, Travis MacGregor. And after the children go to bed, I'll show you how much."

ALSO BY CYNTHIA WOOLF

Bachelors and Babies

Carter

Brides of Homestead Canyon/Montana Sky Series

Thorpe's Mail-Order Bride

Kissed by a Stranger

A Family for Christmas

Bride of Nevada

Genevieve

Brides of the Oregon Trail

Hannah

Lydia

Bella

Eliza

Rebecca

Brides of San Francisco

Nellie

Annie

Cora

Sophia

Amelia

Brides of Seattle

Mail Order Mystery

Mail Order Mayhem

Mail Order Mix-Up

Mail Order Moonlight

Mail Order Melody

Brides of Tombstone

Mail Order Outlaw

Mail Order Doctor

Mail Order Baron

Central City Brides

The Dancing Bride

The Sapphire Bride

The Irish Bride

The Pretender Bride

Destiny in Deadwood

Jake

Liam

Zach

Hope's Crossing

The Stolen Bride

The Hunter Bride

The Replacement Bride

The Unexpected Bride

Matchmaker & Co Series

Capital Bride

Heiress Bride

Fiery Bride

Colorado Bride

The Surprise Brides

Gideon

Tame

Tame a Wild Heart

Tame a Wild Wind

Tame a Wild Bride

Tame A Honeymoon Heart

Tame Boxset

Centauri Series (SciFi Romance)

Centauri Dawn

Centauri Twilight

Centauri Midnight

Singles

Sweetwater Springs Christmas

ABOUT THE AUTHOR

Cynthia Woolf was born in Denver, Colorado and raised in the mountains west of Golden. She spent her early years running wild around the mountain side with her friends.

Their closest neighbor was one quarter of a mile away, so her little brother was her playmate and her best friend. That fierce friendship lasted until his death in 2006.

Cynthia was and is an avid reader. Her mother was a librarian and brought new books home each week. This is where young Cynthia first got the storytelling bug. She wrote her first story at the age of ten. A romance about a little boy she liked at the time.

She worked her way through college and went to work full time straight after graduation and there was little time to write. Then in 1990 she and two friends started a round robin writing a story about pirates. She found that she missed the writing and kept on with other stories. In 1992 she joined Colorado Romance Writers and Romance Writers of America. Unfortunately, the loss of her job demanded she not renew her memberships and her writing stagnated for many years.

In 2000, she saw an ad in the paper for a writers conference being put on by CRW and decided she'd attend. One of her favorite authors, Catherine Coulter, was the keynote speaker. Cynthia was lucky enough to have a seat at Ms. Coulter's table at the luncheon and after talking with her, decided she needed to get back to her writing. She rejoined both CRW and RWA that day and hasn't looked back.

Cynthia credits her wonderfully supportive husband Jim and the great friends she's made at CRW for saving her sanity and allowing her to explore her creativity.

Made in the USA
Monee, IL
07 July 2026